All is Fortune

Other Books by Jonathan Croall

Theatre
John Gielgud: Matinee Idol to Movie Star
In Search of Gielgud: A Biographer's Tale
The Wit and Wisdom (& Gaffes) of John Gielgud
Sybil Thorndike: A Star of Life
Performing Hamlet: Actors in the Modern Age
Performing King Lear: Gielgud to Russell Beale
The Coming of Godot: A Short History of a Masterpiece
Buzz Buzz! Playwrights, Actors and Directors at the National Theatre
Closely Observed Theatre: From the National Theatre to the Old Vic
The National Theatre at Work series
Hamlet Observed
Peter Hall's 'Bacchai'
Inside the Molly House

Film
Forgotten Stars: My Father and the British Silent-Film World
From Silent Idol to *Superman*: The Life and Career of My Father John Stuart

All is Fortune

And Other Theatre Stories

Jonathan Croall

The Book Guild Ltd

First published in Great Britain in 2023 by
The Book Guild Ltd
Unit E2 Airfield Business Park,
Harrison Road, Market Harborough,
Leicestershire. LE16 7UL
Tel: 0116 2792299
www.bookguild.co.uk
Email: info@bookguild.co.uk
Twitter: @bookguild

Copyright © 2023 Jonathan Croall

The right of Jonathan Croall to be identified as the author of this
work has been asserted by him in accordance with the
Copyright, Design and Patents Act 1988.

All rights reserved. No part of this publication may be
reproduced, transmitted, or stored in a retrieval system, in any form or by any means,
without permission in writing from the publisher, nor be otherwise circulated in
any form of binding or cover other than that in which it is published and without
a similar condition being imposed on the subsequent purchaser.

This work is entirely fictitious and bears no resemblance to any persons living or dead.

Typeset in 11pt Minion Pro

Printed and bound in the UK by TJ Books LTD, Padstow, Cornwall

ISBN 978 1915603 814

British Library Cataloguing in Publication Data.
A catalogue record for this book is available from the British Library.

Contents

Curly on My Mind	1
A Visitor	8
Smelling the Coffee Going Forward	17
Sisters	23
'There's This Captain…'	36
Living in the Past	47
A Brief Encounter	64
Unmasked	77
Freedom First	85
All is Fortune	92
Surviving	117
Dateline Moscow	124
A Holiday Humour	130
Carrying On	139
Undercurrents	146
Breaking Through	149
First Thoughts	166
Desperately Seeking Miranda	169
Last Rights	179
Whipping-Girl	185
The Case of the Missing Doll	191

Curly on My Mind

I WAS SURE I would get the part. I reckoned Ado Annie, the girl who 'caint say no', would be a shoo-in. Her story was my story: I'm pretty – or should I say 'purty'? – and sparky, and always up for a bit of fun. Men buzz around me like flies, and I don't always swat them away. On the contrary, I'm like Annie: kissin's my favourite food. With most musicals I've been in, when the lights are low I sure as anything end up in bed with a chorus boy.

During these *Oklahoma!* auditions I made it to the last three for Annie, but no further, darn it. But at least it got me a place in the ensemble. So there I was, Jenny Rivers, the eternal chorus girl, playing one of the all-singing, all-dancing farmers' daughters. Which was fine really: you get to wear great costumes and perform terrific dance routines. Some of the routines were pretty tough going, I can tell you. But Alice was a brilliant choreographer. She worked us seriously hard, we trusted her, and it paid off.

We rehearsed separately from the principals during the first week, and hitched up with them in the second. We began with a warm-up, the whole company singing 'Oklahoma!', the song that ends the show. My, was that some thrill! I could really feel the wind come sweeping down the plain.

Then we worked on the long first scene. I could see straight off the love story between Laurey and Curly was cooking nicely. Sweet, bashful Laurey was played by Joanna Lee, an attractive redhead with a voice to die for and buckets full of charm. But it was Guy Peters as her beau Curly who really got to me. His stage presence was amazing and lit up the gloomy rehearsal room. He had a terrific voice, rich and strong, and full of lovely optimism. The moment he launched into 'Oh What a Beautiful Morning' I was done for.

For the rest of the day I went around in a trance. In the afternoon Guy wooed Joanna with the seductive 'The Surrey with the Fringe on Top'. Oh my God, did I feel envious when she ended up in his arms! After that we girls went through the song-and-dance routine for 'Many a New Day'. Guy's thrilling image kept floating into my mind. Honestly, it was all I could do to remember the moves and the lyrics. But it was his and Joanna's take on 'People Will Say We're in Love' that really blew me away.

We members of the ensemble often went to the pub after rehearsals. That evening Guy and Joanna joined us. When Guy plonked himself down next to me, I tried hard not to blush, clutching my wine glass in an effort to keep calm. To my surprise he took a back seat during the gossip and the anecdotes that followed. He seemed shy and reserved, and said nothing about his work or himself. It was Joanna who took centre-stage, with amusing stories of a disastrous tour of *Hobson's Choice* she'd endured. She and Guy seemed to have exchanged personalities from the ones they were playing on stage. While Guy was quiet and passive, Joanna was bursting with life and keen to know what each of us had done before *Oklahoma!*.

While the others were telling their stories I risked the odd sly glance at Guy. I just swooned all over again at his handsome profile, his gorgeous green eyes, his lovely curly hair. Then it was my turn. I was ashamed to talk about my pathetic career, with only the odd minor comedy role coming between my endless chorus parts. I didn't look at Guy, but I could feel him watching me as I spoke, and somehow this made things worse. Still, I did get a hint of a friendly smile when I finished. That calmed my nerves, though only slightly.

That evening I decided to find out about his past. I looked him up online and discovered he was thirty-eight, once married but now divorced, and had a daughter. He had played heaps of musical leads, including Billy Bigelow in *Carousel*, which is one of my favourite shows. I could just picture him sharing that great duet 'If I Loved You' with young Julie Jordan. I tried to imagine myself as Julie, singing in harmony with Guy, but I couldn't get the image into focus. That night it took me ages to get to sleep.

As rehearsals continued I could think of little else but Guy. My feelings were in disarray, my defences were down, as Ado Annie says. This overwhelming emotion was totally new to me; no man had ever affected me quite like this. Yet we scarcely met during rehearsals, except for exchanging a word by the coffee machine, or a 'See you tomorrow' at the end of the day. And that made me really sad.

But I did have one thrilling moment. One morning we were rehearsing the song-and-dance number 'The Farmer and the Cowman', which has the whole cast performing a brilliant hoe-down. As a bonding exercise Alice asked us to walk round the room, stop at a given signal, and pair off with the nearest member of the opposite sex. I found myself standing next to Guy. 'Howdy, pardner!' he said, in his best Oklahoma accent. I was speechless. Then off we went, me in seventh heaven as he whirled me dizzyingly round the room. That was some bonding, I can tell you!

We repeated the number often that morning. But Alice, damn her, insisted we bond further by having a different partner each time. After that Guy's presence haunted me throughout the day. Later, in the tube going back to my flat, I re-ran in my mind our dance together, and felt again the thrill of being held by him. I began to tap my foot to the rhythm, and mutter the lyrics, until I realised people were staring at me.

Once home I told myself to get real, girl. Nothing romantic or otherwise was going to happen between Guy and me, that was for sure. Why was I even thinking of such a stupid idea? I was used to having a fling with one of the lads in the chorus, enjoying those light-hearted affairs which never last longer than the show. But Guy was a star, and I was nothing but a humble chorus girl. He had shown no interest in me, and I was too mesmerised by him to make any move.

I didn't even know if he had a woman in his life. So the next day I decided to find out. After the rehearsal I followed him through the rush-hour crowds to the tube station. On the train I kept him in sight from my seat in the next carriage. He got off at Putney, and after a short walk he stopped outside a small house, unlocked the door, and went in.

I waited for a while behind a tree on the pavement opposite, hoping he might soon come out. Finally I gave up and left, cursing myself for going on such a bloody fool's errand and behaving like some kind of creepy stalker. I had learned fuck all about Guy.

Then I got a lucky break. The day before the first preview the actress understudying Ado Annie developed laryngitis. Since I already knew the part, the director asked me to act as a temporary cover for the rest of the week. This meant getting into the rehearsal room early the next morning and practising Annie's two songs with Graham, our pianist.

'I Caint Say No' was a breeze; I loved every moment of that witty number. Then Eddie Salter arrived – he was playing Annie's beau Will Parker – and we pitched into our duet 'All or Nuttin'. Eddie had a sharp, humorous voice, just perfect for Will.

'You're getting there!' he said, after a couple of run-throughs.

But I wasn't satisfied. 'Let's give it one more go,' I said.

We were about to start again when I noticed a figure at the back of the room. With a start I realised it was Guy. How long had he been there? And how was I going to cope with him listening? My throat felt suddenly tight. I drank some water to give me time to think. Then I remembered the title of the song, and suddenly I felt determined to give it my all – just for him.

From the start I felt unusually confident in projecting my voice. I knew as I sang that I was catching Annie's perky tone, that I was right inside her character. Her infectious warmth entered my body and took over my voice. I even briefly forgot Guy was there. For those few minutes all seemed right with the world.

As I finished and returned to earth Guy came over. 'That sounded fine, Jenny,' he said. 'You were Annie spot on.' I thanked him, keeping my voice as steady as I could. I was thrilled that he remembered my name and apparently liked my singing. His few quiet words sent my heart dancing.

Yet at the same time I felt tearful, for I knew in my bones that such close contact would be a one-off. Soon I would be back in the chorus line, lost in a crowd of girls, and quite faded from his mind. And so it proved. Annie's understudy recovered in time for the first night. Guy was in truly fine voice and captured the audience's heart, just as he had captured mine.

I had sent him a good-luck card but got no response, which depressed me. During the run of the show we girls would pass him on the way to our dressing rooms. He would give us a general smile, but he never made any sign of remembering me. Yet I continued to be enthralled by his singing, especially 'People Will Say We're in Love'. I would stand in the wings and under my breath softly sing Laurey's part in blissful harmony with him, wishing it would never end.

But it always did, and so did the run. I felt shattered when we went our separate ways. It was the old familiar theatre story: ships that pass in the night. I never worked with Guy again. But I followed his career with secret pride. It was like I possessed him, as if he belonged to me, and me alone.

A Visitor

We actors get all sorts coming round after the show. Friends are always welcome, of course, even if they don't always say what they think. But others can be a real pain. I suppose we all find the occasional oddball in our dressing room. You just have to tolerate them: they go with the territory. But let me tell you about one very strange visitor. This was more than twenty years ago, just before the millennium. Yet it seems like yesterday.

At the time I was lucky enough to be playing Hamlet. We had almost reached the end of a lengthy provincial tour. The production was in modern dress and pleasingly innovative. Our young director was full of bold, imaginative ideas, and the rehearsals had been extremely stimulating. Certain old-fashioned critics disliked her concept of a surveillance-state Elsinore, but it was going down well with our audiences.

A Visitor

One day we were playing in a northern industrial town, in one of those beautiful old Victorian theatres designed by Frank Matcham. After fifteen weeks on the road I was feeling decidedly weary. I was well aware that on some nights I was not doing justice to the great part, and that frustrated and upset me. It was especially tough on matinee days, knowing I'd have to go through another three and a half hours of it in the evening.

This particular Saturday I went through my normal routine in my dressing room between the two performances. I took a quick shower, had a piece of cold chicken, and a small glass of whiskey. I then had a whole hour to myself. I started it by going over any soliloquy I felt needed refreshing. That day I remember working on 'How all occasions do inform against me'. Afterwards I sank into my armchair and took my usual nap before my dresser arrived.

I don't know how long I'd been asleep, but I suddenly became aware of a shadow darkening my vision. As I opened my eyes I was startled to see a stranger standing by my dressing table. It was a young man dressed in Elizabethan costume. I was puzzled. Was this a fan with a warped sense of humour?

'Who are you? What do you want?' I demanded. He made no reply but looked slowly round the room. I studied him closely. He had a fresh, unlined, intelligent face, deep-set piercing brown eyes, a goatee beard, and a large forehead with receding dark hair. I stumbled to my feet and confronted him.

'How the hell did you get past the stage-door keeper?' I demanded.

'Oh, I always find my own way in,' he replied, with a nonchalant air.

His casual manner made me even more irritated. 'Look, will you please leave this minute, and allow me to get ready,' I said. 'I have to be on stage in half an hour.'

He fixed me with a slight smile. 'That gives me ample time.'

'For what?' I said, unwisely. He reached inside his blouse. This alarmed me: was he some kind of lunatic?

'To give you your notes,' he said, drawing out a bulky notebook. He suddenly seemed tired and slumped down on the chair by my dressing table. I noticed for the first time the dark shadows under his eyes. It seemed best to try to humour him.

'Well, make it quick,' I said, returning to my armchair.

'First let me explain,' he began. 'I have been chosen to observe every production of *Hamlet* during this final decade of the century.'

His voice was soft, low, and melodious. I was baffled. 'Chosen by whom exactly?' I enquired.

He ignored my question. 'I have seen every conceivable interpretation of Hamlet himself. Actors of all shapes and sizes and genders, from the inspiring to the downright disgraceful, and everything in between. I never, *ever* want to hear the word Elsinore again. To be quite frank, I've been extremely hard pressed just to keep going this last year. I am completely exhausted, and thoroughly sick at heart. And now, thankfully, I have reached the end of my task. Today is my swansong. So here are my notes.'

If this was a ghost, as I now wondered, despite not

believing in them, he seemed very much flesh and blood. He consulted his notebook.

'In general yours was an interesting performance. I thought you conveyed well Hamlet's energy and wit. But there was a distinct falling-off once you put on your antic disposition. And I'm afraid you failed to heed your own advice to the Players. I'm not saying you tore a passion to tatters, but you certainly didn't speak the speeches trippingly. There were too many unearned pauses between your thoughts. But you made a good end: that final scene with Horatio was very effective, and the death scene was extremely moving.'

'Thank you, that's all very helpful,' I said, making to rise. But he hadn't finished.

'But I fear all is not well with your company,' he continued. 'Your Gertrude played her part with great emotional truth, especially in the closet scene with you, which was very effective. But I'm afraid your Claudius was badly lacking in kingly authority. Ophelia was touching in her madness, but Laertes was worse than colourless. Polonius was merely a caricature, an old dodderer rather than the cunning politician he so obviously is. As for the Ghost...'

He paused and looked up from his notebook. I wondered where he would go next. 'The Ghost was sympathetically played, but he boomed too much, as so often happens. You see...' He paused again, before continuing: 'Horatio, as usual, was worthy but dull, and little more than a feed for Hamlet. Rosencrantz and Guildenstern were barely adequate. But I thought the gravedigger delightful in his humorous exchanges with

Hamlet. To sum up, I have given the production and you a respectable sixty-five per cent rating.'

By now my curiosity was outweighing my annoyance. Keen to know more, I decided to play along with him.

'Tell me, how did you land this unusual job?'

'Oh, you know, by the usual method,' he said, closing his notebook.

'And what exactly is that?'

'Are you really interested?'

'Very much so.'

'Well, at the start of each century auditions are held at the Globe, in front of the Forthcoming Productions panel of the King's Men. For the twentieth century ten of us made it to the shortlist. I was allocated the present decade. Of course, the final decision is always down to Will himself. He's very good at judging us, very aware of each actor's strengths and weaknesses, and of our knowledge of his work.'

I was intrigued. 'So you were one of his company, were you? You must have known him well. Tell me, what was he like? We know so little about him and his life.'

He reflected for a moment. When he spoke it was with a wistful air. 'Yes, I was in the company with him, in his heyday actually. He was a joy to work with, always thoughtful, and generous in the extreme, though he was sometimes inclined to melancholy. He was a canny businessman too, and not at all a bad actor – he played the Ghost in *Hamlet*, you know. He was blessed with a good, deep voice, which enabled him to reach the gallery with ease.'

'Judging from his plays he seems to have read pretty widely.'

'Oh, he did. You'd often find him with his nose in a book or a pamphlet. He was always digging around for ideas for his plays; he was especially keen on the classics for his source material. And once he got down to it he wrote amazingly fast.'

'That's fascinating. And how was he in rehearsals?'

'Oh, absolutely teeming with ideas. He was very adaptable, always ready to come up with a fresh line if something didn't feel right. He had strong views on how scenes should be played. The notes he gave us were wonderfully shrewd and helpful. And in the tavern afterwards he was excellent company, full of jokes and puns. There was no one quite like him when he was on song.'

'I can well imagine,' I said. 'And did you ever meet his wife Anne Hathaway, and his children?'

'Sadly not. When he was in London he kept them well out of the way back in Stratford.'

'It seems odd that he didn't bring his family to London. Did he talk about them much?'

'Hardly at all. Except when Hamnet, one of the twins, died suddenly.'

'Oh, yes. He was very young, wasn't he?'

'Just eleven. It was tragic. Will came back from the funeral very cast down. The boy's death affected him deeply for ages.'

'And soon afterwards he wrote *Hamlet*.'

'Yes. But he didn't invent the name; it belonged to the real Prince of Denmark.'

'I see. Didn't he also have two daughters?'

'Yes. Susanna married a local doctor, and they had a daughter. Will was delighted about that.'

'I must say I find it quite hard to think of him as a grandfather! And the other daughter?'

'Judith? Will told us she was mixed up in a scandal after her marriage to a local vintner. Apparently her husband had an affair with a local woman, who died giving birth to their child, who also died.'

'Poor woman. Talking of which, didn't William himself have a mistress, a woman we know as the Dark Lady?'

He chuckled. 'If he did, he certainly kept us in the dark about her.'

By now I was positively enjoying our conversation. I decided to try another leading question.

'Did he ever say which play he thought was his best? Which work he was most proud of?'

'He did. But I'm afraid that's a question we're not allowed to answer. He was worried that if it got out it would make it harder for people to come to their own opinion.'

'What a shame,' I said. 'It would have been fascinating to know his choice.'

I asked him what William made of the many theories that argued the plays were written by someone else, such as Francis Bacon or Christopher Marlowe or the Earl of Oxford – or even apparently Queen Elizabeth!

'Ah, that old nonsense,' he retorted, roaring with laughter. 'All totally ludicrous. Fairy tales. We actors saw Will working on the stories in the theatre. We listened to him developing his ideas in the tavern in the evenings. He was the one and only author of his plays. No doubt about that whatsoever.'

'What about his travels?' I asked. 'Did he for instance ever go to Italy, where so many of his plays are set?'

'He never mentioned travelling abroad, so I very much doubt it. I suspect he got his knowledge of other countries from books. Anyway,' he smiled, 'I don't want to deprive all those speculating academics of their livelihoods.'

'I see your point. One other question, though. Among the scores of Hamlets you've seen, has there been one actor whose performance stood out?'

He pondered for a moment, stroking his beard. 'In fact, there has been, and a very surprising one it was. I've seen all the best ones during this decade – Branagh, Dillane, Fiennes – but no one quite matched up to a student playing him in a college production I saw up here in the north. It was a uniquely spirited performance, full of youth and intelligence and passion. It was astonishing how such a young man handled the soliloquies so maturely. He conveyed their meaning with absolute clarity. And he was so moving at the end. "The readiness is all" was absolutely heart-breaking.'

By now I had so warmed to my eloquent visitor that I offered him a glass of whiskey. 'Not while I'm on duty, thank you all the same,' he said. 'Besides, I must be on my way. Now the millennium is almost upon us I have to submit my report. Then my task will be complete.'

'So what will you do then?' I enquired, as he rose from his chair.

'Oh, it's much too soon to say. I'm just looking forward to a really good rest, and a holiday away from it all. After that, who knows which play I'll make a pitch for? Certainly one that's less demanding than *Hamlet*. Maybe *The Comedy of Errors*, or perhaps *The Two Gents*? Although I must say I'm tempted to go for *Much Ado*, and that merry war of words.'

'That would be an excellent choice,' I said. 'Benedick is such a wonderful part.' He nodded in agreement, then moved to the door. I felt truly sorry to see him go; there was so much more I was keen to ask him, especially about William. 'Well, I hope you enjoy your rest,' I said. 'It sounds as if you've earned it. And may I say how much I've enjoyed our conversation.'

'I have too,' he replied. 'It's been one of my more pleasurable encounters. Some of the older actors have bored me to death with their... but no, I mustn't start telling tales.'

'I wish you would,' I said.

He laughed but declined. Instead he said, 'May I wish you all the best for the evening performance. And don't forget Hamlet's words of advice to the Players.'

'I'll try not to,' I said. 'I'm already feeling refreshed after your visit.' I got up from my armchair. 'I expect you can see yourself out.'

'Indeed I can,' he replied, smiling. On reaching the door he turned, looked at me in an arresting manner, and intoned in a suddenly resonant voice: 'Remember me.'

As you can see, I have done so. And I always will.

Smelling the Coffee Going Forward

'What's required is a blast of blue-sky thinking,' Cath said. 'We need to prove our chops and play on a bigger pitch. I fear we're conflicted and running out of road. We must leverage our brand more robustly, so we can grow the building's profile.'

Rupert nodded. 'And, er, get ahead of the curve?'

'Precisely.'

Cath Warner was head of the theatre's marketing department. Rupert Tremble was her newly appointed young deputy. Cath continued: 'We need to re-purpose our strategy. The time has come to step up to the plate.'

'And run our concerns up the flagpole?' Rupert added, tentatively.

'Quite. So I've arranged to have a thought-shower this morning with Josh Buzzard.'

'Who?'

'He's the guru who helms the Hot Button workshops. The go-to man for podiuming the high-end issues. I have the narrative oven-ready. I'd like you to come along.'

They met Josh Buzzard at the local hipster CaffèCafé. A tall, fair-skinned man, with a narrow face and hooded eyes, he was dressed all in black denim, with lime-green trainers and a reversed baseball cap over his greying ponytail. 'Good to touch base with you guys,' he said, slipping his Herschel rucksack off his back and ordering a large cappuccino.

'Thanks for sparing the face-time, Josh,' Cath said. 'Great to have you come aboard. This is Rupert, my new deputy.'

'No probs,' he said. 'I'm ready to rock. Just put your peg in the ground and we'll punch through the mix.'

'OK, let's bring you into the loop,' Cath began. 'We have issues around our marketing strategy and customer interface. We badly need to re-architecturise and progress them, raise the bar early doors, and big up our ideas management. Otherwise we're toast. So we're looking to you to come up with a toolkit and synopsise the how.'

'No worries, Cath,' Josh replied, curving his bony fingers round his cappuccino. 'I'm happy to concretise a pre-conversation, to smell the coffee going forward. That's what I'm tasked to do at Hot Button. So hey, why don't we kick around a few ideas, and see if they have legs.'

'Brilliant!' said Cath, taking a bite out of her almond croissant.

'Absolutely!' Rupert agreed, nibbling his chocolate brownie.

'Here's my elevator pitch,' Josh began, adjusting his ponytail. 'Your first step must be to move the needle by freeing up your current route-one repertoire. At the moment it's just a one-way ticket to yawnsville. Your risk-averse diet of Ayckbourn, Coward, Priestley, Agatha Christie, and all those trad productions of Will Shakespeare is so last century, and not good optics. There's no wiggle room to stage work which interrogates your audience and takes them out of their comfort zone. To impact your demographic you need to man up and factor in a new conversation.'

Cath nodded. 'Point taken. But that's just the low-hanging fruit. What should we strategise instead?'

Josh wiped a touch of froth off his upper lip. 'You know what? The trick is to roll out a repertoire of the work of edgier, in-your-face playwrights, to partner up with the ones coming down the pike who embody the zeitgeist and get all the shout-outs. That way you'll create a tingle factor and hit the sweet spot. The pinch point will be to privilege writers at the top of their game, the kind who can take you on a journey landmarked with marquee moments.'

'That's all good,' Cath replied, 'but it's quite a stretch. The question is, will it cut through and ensure enough bums on seats? Maybe some of the old guard should still be in the mix? Otherwise there's a real danger of blowback.'

'And of falling south of our target,' Rupert ventured cautiously.

Josh laughed. 'Hey, you can still Shakespearianise your repertoire. That's where your agency and soft power lie. But here's a heads-up: the old texts no longer have traction; they need deconstructing and unpicking. You have to segue into a must-see bucket list, and task your writers to author a bunch of more robust, immersive iterations of the plays, with plenty of rubbing points.'

'I clock that,' Cath said. 'But can you drill down a little further?'

'Sure. Here's a few game-changers for starters. Have your theatre stage *The Tempest* in the Met Office, with Prospero channelling Michael Fish. Re-imagine *The Taming of the Shrew* as a story of sexual harassment by Petruchio. How about a mash-up of *Hamlet* and *The Comedy of Errors*? Maybe you could set *The Merchant of Venice* in a credit-union office up north, with Shylock as the company's CEO. Or turn *King Lear* into a piece of verbatim theatre, using testimonies by the homeless living in an East End hovel.'

Cath frowned. 'That's pretty high-tariff stuff you've put on the table. But will our audience unpack it? I fear they might sunset such ideas, or just accuse us of virtue-signalling. And won't we be in danger of being cancelled for being woke?'

'And then it's a no-show,' Rupert suggested.

'Oh, those type of projects will stack up all right,' Josh replied. 'They're the kind that make Shakespeare a turbo-charged, water-cooler figure. But to future-proof them you have to factor in your creatives from the get-go, partner up with the kind of iconic theatre-makers who can journeyise their characters and guarantee you a wow factor. That has to be the pivotal driver for upticking your renewal.'

Cath thought for a moment. 'OK, but supposing we upskill the repertoire along those lines. The challenge would then be to drive up our core customer base. And I have to fess up: that's an area so above my pay grade.'

Josh leant forward in his metal chair. 'Here's the thing. The key is to outreach to your end users. Give them a sense of ownership, of inclusivity. In order to monetise your product, you need to free up and recalibrate your resources. So look, if you want to cross the line numberwise and achieve a spike, the pull factor would be to headquarterise the theatre as a community hub.'

'Make it a portal to drive up your footfall?' Cath suggested.

'Exactly. Don't worry about over-sharing. Incentivise all those fashionistas and outliers to make chilling out there the new normal. Remember to foreground plenty of shoe-leather research around the estates, to reach Generation F: they're your future audience.'

'But what about our grant?' Rupert interjected, with growing confidence. 'Right now we're time-rich and cash-poor.'

'Look, if you're after a roar scenario, you need to take a granular approach and front up the problem,' Josh said. 'You have to do the hard yards, and action the networking and schmoozing. Weaponise those activities front and centre twenty-four seven, and they'll be sure to fly.'

'And how do we do that?' Cath asked.

'It's a no-brainer. Just summonise a key player with the right interpersonal life skills, someone who can think outside the box, who can lean in. Have them showboat your assets, furrow into the stakeholders in your community, and viralise your needs offline. That way you'll be coming down the road to the future.'

Cath drained her coffee cup. 'There's some smoking-hot thoughts there, Josh. Some great tropes. I love it that they have such great swagger value.'

'Hope you can birth some of them,' Josh replied, reaching for his rucksack. 'And now I must head over to Shoreditch for my Motivating Your Creatives workshop.'

'Sure thing,' Cath said. 'Anyway, thanks for a great session. We'll find some down-time soon, war-game those ideas of yours, and let them marinate a little. Then perhaps we could diaryise another brush-by and push the envelope again?'

'Tick, tick,' Josh replied, getting to his feet. 'Just give us a bell.' He donned his baseball cap. 'Laters.'

'Laters,' Cath and Rupert replied, in unison.

Sisters

(All e-mail addresses have been omitted and names changed to protect the privacy of the correspondents.)

From Polly Champion – Dear Greg Warner, I understand you are the Literary Manager of the theatre. I hope you might be interested in my play *Leaving Oakbridge*, which I attach. It's based on Chekhov's *Three Sisters*, updated to our time, and set in the kind of small West Country town which might be familiar to you. It's been read by a writer friend of mine, Danny Williams, who liked it a lot, and thought it would suit your studio theatre. I look forward to hearing from you in due course. Regards, Polly Champion

*

From Polly Champion – Dear Alice Bradbury, I gather you are Greg Warner's assistant. Some five weeks ago I sent him a play called *Leaving Oakbridge*. I realise he will have many other scripts to consider. But I would be grateful if you could confirm that he has at least received mine. Regards, Polly Champion

*

From Polly Champion – Dear Alice Bradbury, I am worried that my play sent to you eight weeks ago has got lost. Could you please confirm that I am mistaken. Regards, Polly Champion

*

From Alice Bradbury – Dear Ms Champion, My apologies for not acknowledging your play sooner. I have now found it on our shelves. Mr Warner receives a large number of unsolicited scripts for consideration, so it may be some time before he gets round to reading yours. If you don't hear from us within six months, please send us a stamped addressed A4 envelope, and we will return it to you. Yours sincerely, Alice Bradbury, Assistant to Mr Warner

*

From Polly Champion – Dear Danny, As you suggested, I sent my play off to Greg Warner. After two months of deafening silence his assistant eventually acknowledged it with a standard 'Don't ring us' letter. Since then, total silence, which is really frustrating. As you have been reading scripts for the theatre, would you feel able to put in a word? Or is that stretching our friendship too far? You'd be doing me a massive favour. As ever, Polly

*

From Danny Williams – Dear Greg, A small request. Last night I was contacted by a young woman I know slightly called Polly Champion. She told me she sent you a play several months ago, and is concerned not to have had any response. I gather it's based on Chekhov's *Three Sisters* and is called *Leaving Oakbridge*. I imagine it's sitting in your slush pile like all the other unsolicited ones. It sounded interesting. Might I read it for you? As ever, Danny

*

From Greg Warner – Dear Ms Champion, I spent last evening reading your play. It's a very original work, and I was held by it throughout. I think you have caught the zeitgeist spot on, and your portrait of the three women stuck in the dreary provincial backwater and yearning to move to London is a very sympathetic one. I especially like your skilful use of time shifts, and those surreal dream sequences. I like too the idea of an abstract set reflecting the emptiness of the sisters' lives. I have a number of criticisms but would be very keen to discuss them and the play with you. Would you care to drop by the theatre one day next week? Just fix a time with my assistant Alice Bradbury. Warm regards, Greg Warner, Literary Manager

*

From Polly Champion – Dear Greg, I found our meeting yesterday really valuable. I am thrilled you are willing to help me revise the play, and that, all being well, you will recommend it to your artistic director. I appreciate your warning that Simon Anderson has very conservative tastes. I was introduced to him in the bar last year, and that soon became very clear. I have to say, between ourselves, I didn't take to him at all.

Can I just summarise the main changes you suggested and that I agreed with?

I need to cut two of the minor characters to make the cast size more manageable. Six is the absolute maximum you can afford. I agreed that Debbie and Mr Candle were dispensable.

Olivia and Imogen are well-rounded and sympathetic characters, but I should give more depth to Millie and her plight. Her emotions should be stronger, her alienation from the local people more marked. This is essentially a feminist play.

There are too many dream sequences – you thought Olivia's Hyde Park fantasy could go. And the final act needs tightening up, to avoid losing the momentum.

Alexander's part is somewhat underwritten: his underlying affection for his sisters is not obvious enough. You also question whether being a librarian is a job that fits in with his philistine personality.

All this is really helpful. I shall get to work straight away, and hope to send you an improved version before too long. With many thanks, Polly

*

From Greg Warner – Dear Polly, You have done an excellent job on the re-write. I'm impressed that you have responded so positively to my criticisms. I have passed the new version on to Simon Anderson and plan to discuss it with him on Friday, when he and I will be thinking about next year's programme. I think this will be the first real test of his agreement to include more new writing in our programme, especially by women, whom we have seriously neglected up to now. I have suggested to him that we devote a month in the summer to staging promising work in a series of productions without decor, but so far I'm not making much headway. I do feel we're badly in need of provocative, experimental work like yours, which investigates so strongly our divided society. All the best, Greg

*

From Simon Anderson – Dear Greg, Let me just summarise my criticism of Ms Champion's *Leaving Oakbridge*.

She makes little attempt to disguise the fact that Oakbridge is actually our own community. Our audience will resent this. Her picture of the town is unreasonably harsh and clearly prejudiced, especially the portraits of the hard-working businessmen who provide the backbone of its life.

The three women talk endlessly about longing to leave Oakbridge, but there is no sense that they are prepared to put the town and its need for development before their personal ambition. There needs to be a great deal more positive thinking from them if we are to care about their situation.

If Olivia really wants to improve her pupils' lot, she should be applying for a more senior post in her school. Similarly, Imogen needs to reflect on her depressed attitude while working for the council, rather than continually moaning about all the paperwork she has to deal with. As for Millie, given the cuts to the parks budget, she should count herself lucky to have held on to her gardening job.

I am not at all in favour of the abstract sets that the writer is calling for. These are bound to alienate our audience, who take delight in visual beauty and realistic sets, which give a clear and immediate sense of where the action is taking place.

I disapprove of the dream sequences, which are not only obscure but horribly out of key with the other scenes. They belong to another play, the kind that is staged *ad nauseam* in London for a metropolitan elite audience. Our town's loyal theatregoers would not respond well to such pseudo-intellectual fare.

Given these fundamental objections, I feel strongly that this is not a script we should consider taking forward. Please inform Ms Champion of my decision. Cordially, Simon

*

From Greg Warner – Dear Polly, I attach Simon Anderson's comments on your play. You will be as disappointed as I am by his criticisms. They quite fail to take into account the original nature of your play, and its sympathetic picture of the sisters' situation. But he obviously feels strongly about your work, however misguidedly, and I'm afraid the decision is ultimately his. I'm sorry this has in the end been a fruitless and frustrating experience for you. I do hope you'll be able to place *Leaving Oakbridge* with a more sympathetic theatre. You deserve better treatment than we have been able to give you. With apologies again and best wishes, Greg

*

From Polly Champion – Dear Greg, I have to say I was very surprised at Simon Anderson's dismissive critique. It seems to me blinkered in the extreme, and to betray an astonishing degree of ignorance of what the play is about. I was also surprised you were unwilling to defend my play, after having previously praised it so strongly. Having worked very hard to revise it in the light of your helpful criticisms, I feel thoroughly let down. But I certainly don't intend to give up. I just need to think about where I go from here. Regards, Polly

*

From Greg Warner – Dear Polly, I fully understand your anger and disappointment. Between ourselves, I quite agree that Simon's comments are ludicrously wide of the mark, and all too reflective of his lack of vision. I did try to make him think again, arguing that your kind of play would help to attract the younger, more diverse audience which we badly need. But I can see there is little hope of changing his mind. Anyway, I do hope you carry on writing, as you clearly have talent. If it helps, I'd be happy to comment informally on any future ideas you may have, and perhaps suggest a more sympathetic venue. I feel it's the least I can do in the circumstances. Best, Greg

*

From Polly Champion – Dear Greg, Thanks for your offer. I would in fact like to talk to you about an idea that has been lurking at the back of my mind. Could we meet for a coffee one day, though preferably not at the theatre? Best, Polly

*

From Greg Warner – Dear Polly, I have thought long and hard about what you suggested at our meeting yesterday. I can quite understand your bitterness, and your desire to take revenge. I was of course shocked and completely taken aback by your story. Whatever his faults, I didn't take Simon for that kind of man. If that's how he behaved that evening at the bar it was obviously quite unacceptable. But I advise you not to take such a drastic step without considering the implications extremely carefully. To start with, I doubt whether he would reconsider a play that he so clearly dislikes. Secondly, if you then decide to expose his behaviour publicly, it is bound to have a damaging effect and put a stain on the theatre's reputation, and of course on that of his family. Do you really want this to happen? I know you are determined to get your work staged, but this seems to me the wrong way to go about it. It's the sort of action that could easily rebound on you, to the detriment of your desire to forge a career in the theatre. So please, please reconsider this course of action. Yours in hope, Greg

*

From Polly Champion – Dear Greg, Sorry, but I don't think you understand how disturbed I was by what happened in the bar. I don't just mean his pervy behaviour, but his assumption that he could get away with it because of his status. This is what we women have to put up with all the time from men in powerful positions. People say we shouldn't take it so seriously, that we should be more 'robust' – that ghastly word. In this way we are seen as the ones to blame for this kind of behaviour, and it's the men who are the victims if we expose their behaviour. Well, now that more women are daring to speak out, I'm emboldened to do so myself. But as I made clear, I'm prepared to remain silent on condition he agrees to stage my play in the studio. I am writing to him today to that effect. OK, it's blatant blackmail, but I'm quite easy with that. My play is my priority. Yours, Polly

*

From Polly Champion – Dear Mr Anderson, Greg Warner has passed on to me your comments about *Leaving Oakbridge*. I was disappointed that you failed to appreciate the play's basic intention or sympathise at all with the despair of the sisters. Obviously you are looking at it from a purely male viewpoint, and therefore a distorted one. I am not surprised that women find it virtually impossible to get their work staged in your theatre. So can I ask you to have another think about my play? Perhaps you could send it out it to a female reader for an informed second opinion? Incidentally, I have been reflecting on our encounter at the theatre bar last month, and your inappropriate behaviour. I have so far kept this harassment to myself, but now that similar cases are coming to light I am seriously considering speaking out about it. Yours sincerely, Polly Champion

*

From Simon Anderson – Dear Greg, I attach a disturbing message from Ms Champion. Needless to say, nothing of the kind took place. I do remember the meeting, and thinking what an opinionated young woman she was. I may have had a couple of drinks, and I seem to remember we had a bit of a set-to about our programme last year, and in particular the Priestley play. But I'm sure I never laid a finger on her – and nor would I want to. My first thought on receiving her threat was to contact my lawyer. But having slept on it overnight, I've decided to call her bluff. I'm certainly not going to yield to such blatant blackmail. I don't want to reply in writing to her accusation. But it would be extremely helpful if you could talk to her personally on my behalf and make it quite clear that I totally deny her allegation, and that I have no intention of seeking a further opinion about her play. With thanks for your support, Simon

*

From Greg Warner – Dear Polly, I'm sorry that we weren't able to speak yesterday. Let's do so when you're back from your holiday in Italy. Meanwhile Mr Anderson has asked me to tell you that he flatly denies your allegation and will not budge on his decision about your play. I do hope the break will give you a chance to view this matter more calmly, and see where your best interests lie. With all good wishes, Greg

*

From Greg Warner – Dear Simon, I have just heard the sad news about Ms Champion who, while on holiday in Italy, was one of the victims of the terrible Naples train crash. I was informed of this yesterday by a phone call from Canada from her sister Adrienne, who left a message on my phone. When I eventually spoke to her she was understandably very upset. She wanted to know if we still had the script of Polly's play. I explained that we had regrettably turned it down and returned it to her. She then asked if we could meet when she comes over for the funeral. I'm not clear at this stage if she is aware of the more personal matter, so I think it would be best if I did see her, and try to find out what she knows. Regards, Greg

*

From Simon Anderson – Dear Greg, Thank you for passing on the news. Of course I was most sorry to hear about her death. I agree that a meeting with the sister makes sense. If the other matter comes up, please make sure she is aware of my response. Thanks. Simon

*

From Greg Warner – Dear Simon, I met Polly Champion's sister Adrienne yesterday. I am afraid she is all too aware of the alleged incident. Apparently Polly wrote a detailed account of it in her diary, which Adrienne found in her flat, along with the playscript. She showed me a copy of the relevant diary page, which is clearly incriminating. She is very angry – it seems she and Polly had been close – and is seriously considering going public with the story after the funeral. Thinking on my feet, I told her about our Emerging Talent Month next summer. I suggested we might be able to come to some arrangement whereby she would agree not to publicise the matter, in exchange for you agreeing to stage Polly's play. I intimated that you might be open to such an idea, and that you appreciated the importance of being seen to support new writing. Knowledge of this unfortunate matter would then be confined to the two of us. Best, Greg

*

From Simon Anderson – Dear Greg, Although I'm by no means sure the Emerging Talent Month will bear fruit, I think in the circumstances we should push ahead with it. I believe I can persuade the board to back it on an experimental basis. I also think we should present the inclusion of Ms Champion's play in the project as our tribute to a young playwright tragically cut off in her prime. Have a word with Marketing, and get them to come up with a good, punchy slogan along those lines. Meanwhile please contact the sister again and let her know our decision. Gratefully, Simon

*

From Greg Warner – Dear Simon, Thank you for your understanding of this delicate situation, and for agreeing to include Ms Champion's play in the Emerging Talent Month project. I'm sure it will help to widen our audience base, and encourage more young writers, especially women, to show us their work. I do think this is the best way to ensure her damaging accusation does not go beyond the two of us. I'm sure you won't regret your decision. Regards, Greg

'There's This Captain...'

As LADY LUCK would have it I had nothing in the pipeline at that moment. Not so much as a whisper. Unfortunately it was a fair while since yours truly had trodden the boards. Much too long for an experienced old trouper like me.

Luckily my sister Eleanor, who's on the admin side of theatre, is a dab hand at what she calls 'networking'. The other day she got a bell from a director friend, Anna Hopcraft. Apparently she was having a spot of bother in Bristol with a production of *Twelfth Night*. It seems the actor doubling as the Captain and the Priest had suddenly fallen ill, and the budget didn't run to understudies. So Anna was desperately phoning around to find someone to take over. Eleanor, bless her cotton socks, immediately thought of little old me. Anyway, to cut a long story short, I agreed to play the knight in shining armour and step into the breach – or should I say breeches? Anyway, before you

'There's This Captain...'

could say Henry Irving I was off in a flash on my rescue mission.

I used the train journey to practise one of my many skills, which is to dream up a detailed backstory for my character. Or characters, in this case. As you know, the Captain and the Priest each have just one scene, but they both play a crucial role in the story. If you remember, in the second scene the Captain comes on with Viola after their ship has been hit by a storm and sunk to the bottom of the briny. He's the one who tells her the good news that her twin brother Sebastian might have survived the shipwreck. He also spells out the amorous goings-on in Illyria between Olivia and the duke Orsino (a part I played myself in my golden youth, to some considerable effect, I was told).

For his backstory I decided the Captain was Illyria born and bred, and had gone to sea after his business and his marriage had failed. Originally a vintner, he had fallen foul of the Customs and Excise over a notorious smuggling affair. Afterwards he had run a popular inn by the sea, called the Cakes and Ale – a neat allusion, this, though I say so myself. After sailing on the high seas, he was returning to Illyria to attend his only daughter's wedding. Viola refers to (and I quote) 'his good mind and fair behaviour', and it's clear from the 'gentle help' (her words again) which he gives her that he's a people person, as indeed am I, so a spot of clever casting there.

Then there's the Priest, whom I've decided is called Dominic. His words are key to the final revelation and the play's happy ending. It's he who provides the evidence that Olivia and Sebastian have tied the knot. And what a wonderfully poetic description of the marriage service the Bard gives him – and in just a few lines!

Actually it's the Priest's reference to his watch that gave me the vital clue to his character: I see him as disciplined, reliable, a bit pompous, but a great friend to the poor. Although he has no more lines, Shakespeare leaves him on stage for the rest of the action. This will give me the opportunity to bring out his finer qualities through my body language. Physical theatre is a bit of a speciality of mine these days, one of many strings to my acting bow.

Anyway, arriving in Bristol that Sunday evening, and having found my digs – a bit outside the city, but beggars can't be choosers – I had a brief tipple with young Anna, insisting it was my treat. She was a small woman and, to be honest, no great beauty. Red T-shirt, black jeans, white trainers and purple hair – all very trendy, I suppose. Not that I minded that, as she was perfectly friendly. Straight away it was: 'I can't thank you enough, Stephen, for filling in at such short notice.'

Eleanor had told me Anna was well known for her 'ground-breaking ideas'. I'm pretty much the same, so we were obviously a team made in heaven. I offered to share my imaginative ideas about the Captain with her. But it turned out she had a meeting with the lighting designer shortly, and suggested we leave that discussion until tomorrow's rehearsal. Fair enough, I thought. After treating myself to a spot of the amber nectar and a pizza – my usual bacon and pineapple, for my sins – I went back to my digs and got stuck into jamming my lines into the old brain.

'There's This Captain...'

In the morning, as is my wont, I turned up early for rehearsal. I like to absorb the atmosphere of any new venue, to be 'in tune with the vibes', as the saying goes. Also it gave me a chance to tackle Anna about the Captain's costume. But then she said, 'I'm sorry, I quite forget to tell you, this is a modern-dress production.' Which, as you can imagine, came as a bit of a surprise.

'Ah,' I said, 'so I suppose it's a matter of the full naval uniform?'

She paused for a moment, then said, 'Let's have a talk with Rodney later.' (Rodney is apparently our designer.) I reckoned I shouldn't grumble; I quite fancied a smart naval outfit. Although as it's been in the water for many hours it's probably shrunk somewhat.

The church hall was even shabbier than the ones I usually rehearse in, and that's saying something. It looked like the wreck of the Hesperus, if I may use a nautical image. But no problem there; I'm well known for being quick to adapt to any environment. The other actors greeted me warmly and thanked me for coming to the rescue of Penny, the tall actress playing Viola. She herself came over to say how much she looked forward to working with me. Naturally I returned the compliment. It's a golden rule of mine to be on good terms from the start with my fellow thespians.

Lack of work recently has meant I've put on a few pounds round the old tummy. So the traditional warm-up – the breathing exercises and stretching and running about and tossing bean bags around – left me a trifle breathless. Anna then sensibly suggested we go straight into my scene, to get it up to speed with the others. I said casually that I would be off the book as soon as we had blocked the scene. I guessed this would impress her. However it turned out she didn't believe in blocking but preferred to let the actors, as she put it, 'play it as you feel it'. This was a new idea to me, but I was definitely game, as it would give me more freedom to explore the Captain's complex character.

On the train coming down I had hit on a simple but, in my humble opinion, dramatically effective plan: I would enter carrying the clearly exhausted Viola on my back. But having got a shufti at Penny, a somewhat hefty lady who rather towered above me, I hastily dropped that idea. Happily a neat alternative sprang to mind. I would enter first alone, roam around the stage surveying the scene, bring out a pair of binoculars, spot Viola in the distance, wave to her, dash offstage, and re-enter supporting her by the arm.

I put the idea to Anna, who was clearly startled by its ingenuity. She said it was an interesting thought, which we could try later, but for now Viola and I should just walk on together and go straight into her line 'What country, friend, is this?' Quite frankly this seemed a bit of a cliché, but I kept my powder dry, if you catch my drift.

Then, for the moment when I tell Viola that Sebastian may have survived the shipwreck, I had a flash of inspiration. Since this is a very vivid speech, I put it to Anna that I should suit the action to the word – I thought a Hamlet allusion would go down well here – and mime Sebastian binding himself to the mast, riding the waves, and so forth. I reckoned this would give the action some much-needed oomph.

Anna asked Penny if she was happy with my suggestion, to which the dear girl generously replied, 'We could give

'There's This Captain...'

it a go.' So when we re-played the lines I pulled out all the stops. This caused quite a stir among the watching actors, which was encouraging. It's my guess that, with all this Method malarkey doing the rounds, they're a bit out of touch with my more virile style of acting.

I was grateful to Penny for supporting my idea. During the coffee break I sat down next to her to express my gratitude. She seemed a trifle distracted, so as a thank-you I decided then and there to share my Captain's backstory with her. 'That's an interesting take on him,' she said, stirring her coffee. Encouraged by her approval, I offered to create a backstory for Viola. But Penny thought it would be better if she did that herself. I suppose she had a point; she seems a very down-to-earth, practical lady. But flexibility is my middle name, so I tactfully changed the subject.

Anna then decided we should do a run-through of the first act. This gave me a chance to see how Trevor played Orsino in the opening scene, and how he coped with that famous speech, 'If music be the food of love'. I wondered how it would compare with my own highly romantic interpretation all those years ago. I must say I was disappointed: his Orsino was a very camp character, constantly flirting with Curio and the other lords, who lounged about his court in an unnecessarily suggestive manner. To my mind this was a mistake: Orsino is clearly a noble duke, and totally smitten with Olivia. Granted, he's noticeably keen on flowers, but that doesn't in itself make him a gentleman of the gay persuasion. Not that I have anything against their community, you understand – despite all those little moustaches.

Before we started on my scene Anna asked for a quick word. She suggested that, as I was still on the book, it would be best if, until I was sure of my lines, the Captain held back on the physical actions. Actually I had found it a touch tricky having to mime to my heart's content while clutching my Arden edition. I could see her suggestion made sense, so when we played the scene again I duly obliged. To my way of thinking the result was a little flat, but I reckoned that once I knew my lines, I could put all the actions back.

On the Friday we reached the final act, in which the Priest makes his crucial intervention. It's what I like to call an identity scene, where everyone discovers who everyone else really is. The dear old Bard has used this device more than once, but to my mind it still goes down a treat. I had the Priest's revelatory speech word-perfect, so when it came to my big moment in the sun it went off without a hitch. This left me free before the next rehearsal to develop ideas about his fascinating character.

For starters, I felt it would make sense if I came on earlier than is marked in the text, at the same time as Olivia and her attendants. This would give me a chance to establish my priestly credentials within her household. I also thought an altar could be built in one corner of the stage, which to be honest is a tad short of realistic scenery. I could then kneel there in prayer, and perhaps spray some incense around with a *thurible*. (My uncle's a well-respected Catholic priest in a church in Surbiton, so I'm more than familiar with the terminology.) Then Olivia could suddenly spot me ('O welcome, Father') and bring me forward to back up her story. I suggested all

'There's This Captain...'

this to Anna over my egg-and-cress sandwich during the lunch break. Although she was busy on her laptop, and obviously had a lot on her plate – though no sandwiches! – she promised to make a note of it and get back to me. I must say she seems very receptive to my creative ideas.

In the afternoon we did a run-through of the act, for the moment leaving my entrance as it was in the text. The following Monday it was back to the opening scenes. By then I'd got friendly with a very pretty assistant stage manager, Charlotte by name, who had booked me in to see Anna at the end of the day. I'd made a list of my ideas so we could have a good old chinwag.

But once the other actors had left she dropped a bit of a bombshell. 'Change of plan,' she said: she had decided the Captain should be female. It took me several moments to absorb this unexpected news. But I quickly pulled myself together and told her, trying to keep it light-hearted, that playing in drag wasn't really in my armoury of skills. 'No,' she said, 'you misunderstand me. I think the part should be played by a woman.'

As you can imagine this left me temporarily lost for words. She said she realised this must come as a bit of a blow. But she wanted to do what she called 'a bit of gender-swapping', and this seemed the only possibility; in fact, she had already found an actress to take over the Captain. Before I could get my thoughts together she added that she'd been reflecting on my ideas about the Priest, and felt his speech would have more impact if he gave it from the centre-stage balcony of Olivia's house.

This I quickly realised made a lot of sense, reflecting his key role in the story. It would also go some way to make up for losing the part of the Captain. So, professional to my fingertips, I said I accepted her decision and would focus on giving her a Priest to remember. She was obviously relieved and thanked me for taking the news so well.

I was not on the call sheet for the following day, but I turned up anyway. I wanted to see how my replacement coped, and to show there were no hard feelings on my part. I had spent the weekend trying to ponder the notion of a female Captain, but to be perfectly honest I thought it was political correctness gone mad.

Anyway, before the rehearsal began there was an earnest discussion about whether the newcomer, Jemima, was a woman playing a man, or simply a woman who had risen through the naval ranks, as Anna pointed out they do these days. Jemima thought she might be trans-sexual, but I'm glad to say this was obviously a step too far, even for Anna.

To be quite candid, after they had run the scene a couple of times, I felt Anna had made a serious mistake. Far be it from me to say so publicly, but Jemima just didn't come up to scratch as an authority figure, as a Captain obviously should. Knowing what sailors are like – I've got a nephew in the Merchant Navy who can tell a tale or two – I just couldn't picture her giving orders to a crew of sea-hardened men. To make matters worse she was on the small side, and hardly came up to Penny's shoulder. The unfortunate result was that Viola dominated a scene that should obviously have been equally balanced. Still, you have to be grateful for small mercies: the new Captain might have been black. Imagine!

'There's This Captain...'

There was only time for one more run-through of the Priest's scene. My costume was still being worked on, so I borrowed a black cloak from the stage manager, to give a hint of my occupation. Although Anna had clearly liked my ideas about the earlier entry and the side altar, she felt it would be better if I didn't appear until summoned by Olivia. I could then emerge on to the central balcony. I have a reputation for being quick off the mark, and I immediately saw that in that central elevated position all eyes would be upon me.

In my digs I had been practising different ways of delivering the speech. I finally fixed on the tone my uncle uses when he's giving one of his sermons in Surbiton. It's a kind of steady drone that echoes movingly round the church. I adopted this when it came to my opening line, 'A contract of eternal bond of love', and continued at the same pitch until the end.

Anna had critical notes for some of the actors. Happily I was not among them, which I thought a good sign. But my satisfaction didn't last long. That night at my digs I had a phone call from Anna. She informed me that the actor I had replaced had recovered much quicker than expected and was able to return to the company before the previews. She said it had been a frightfully difficult decision, but she was going to have to honour his original contract, and so would be forced to release me.

This, of course, was quite a setback. However, she apologised profusely, and thanked me for being such a helpful and understanding replacement. She also promised to consider finding me a role in one of her forthcoming productions. I must admit this did make up a little for my disappointment. I asked her what she had in mind. She said nothing concrete right now, but she'd be in touch as soon as something suitable came up.

This is the nature of theatre. It's a tough old world. But we thespians get used to such ups and downs. Mind you, as those who know me will testify, I'm not the type to let a little setback like this get me down. It's happened before and it'll happen again. You just have to take it on the chin, and carry on. Pick yourself up, dust yourself down, and start all over again, as the song has it. That's my motto, and it's what I'm widely known for in the profession.

Living in the Past

TEN MILES TO go, and I'm starting to panic. I can feel my hands shaking on the wheel. What am I doing? Why has he suddenly summoned me after such a long silence? I need to steady my nerves.

I stop in a lay-by and get out of the car. I try to calm myself down by surveying the sun-swept Sussex countryside. But all I can see is that face, that solid body, that unique voice. The trouble is, when I walk into his house, I'll not just be meeting Wallace Herrick but also Coriolanus, Volpone, Captain Shotover, Galileo – not to mention the Scottish Gentleman. Of course, as I keep telling myself, actors are only ordinary human beings. But when you've been transported by them in the theatre, as I so often have, it's hard to banish the magic and mystery that they evoke.

I hear the Cowardly Lion in me putting his persuasive case: 'Go on, Edmund, turn back, there's still time. A puncture, a family accident, a gas leak in your flat. It would only need a quick phone call. Why cause yourself unnecessary embarrassment?' But then I hear the insistent voice of the Intrepid Researcher: 'Are you insane? This is a great figure in the British theatre! Are you seriously going to pass up the chance to write his Life?'

So I drive on, the panic subsiding a little. I finally reach Hamscombe, an attractive village tucked into the folds of the South Downs. I find The Willows down a pretty lane off the high street. It's a large, handsome, whitewashed house, with a neat front garden full of roses of many colours, and wisteria covering the walls.

The door is opened by a small, trim, middle-aged woman, with short auburn hair, a mauve trouser suit and a watery smile. 'Hello, I'm Penny Carter,' she says. 'You must be Edmund Galloway.' Her manner is firm, her confident voice very Home Counties. She sweeps me briskly into the house and shows me into the sitting room, adding, 'I'll go and play Hunt the Herrick.'

I gaze around the dark, cluttered room. Every inch of wall is covered with posters of past theatrical glories. On top of a piano stands a collection of framed signed photos of actors, famous in days gone by. Books are overflowing from the shelves on to the floor, heaped in untidy piles among batches of theatre programmes and battered copies of *Who's Who in the Theatre*. Above the fireplace, communing with Yorick's skull, hangs a portrait of a youthful Hamlet, which I quickly identify as Herrick.

Penny Carter returns from her search. 'Wally's out in the garden, working in the gazebo. It used to belong to Ivor Novello, or so he likes to tell people. He claims it's the best place to learn his lines. We'll have coffee out there: do come through to the kitchen while I make it.'

We pass along a corridor filled with framed sketches of costume designs. As we reach the kitchen I ponder on her role in this encounter. Is she part of the vetting committee? If so, is she an ally or a foe? As she puts the kettle on she seems to have read my mind. 'I'm an old friend of the family. I've been organising Wally's work since his wife Rosalind died last year. No doubt you were surprised to hear from him after all this time.'

'I certainly was,' I reply. 'To be honest I'd rather given up on the idea.'

'Since Rosalind's death he's been looking back at their past together. But he's also started to consider the future. So he's been thinking again about your biography idea. But of course he's worried.'

'About what exactly?'

She puts the coffee cups on a tray. 'That you might dish the dirt on him.'

'What dirt is that?'

'Oh, there's always something, isn't there? Even when there isn't, if you know what I mean. No, what he's after is a book that will fix his reputation for posterity.'

'I'm sure the kind I write would do that,' I reply. 'I want to tell his story properly, spell out his achievement in full measure – if that doesn't sound too pompous.'

'Not at all. But he's uncertain how far he can trust you to do that.'

'I hoped my track record would speak for itself. For instance, my biography of William Hall. Has he read the copy I sent him?'

She laughs quietly. 'I very much doubt it. Anyway, come and meet him.'

*

Walking across the spacious back garden, we approach Wallace Herrick standing in the gazebo. He's offering the world his celebrated profile, his chin squarely up, his eyes closed as he speaks his lines. Becoming aware of our presence, he stops, opens one eye, gives me a sideways glance, then asks Penny, 'A guest? At this hour?'

She sighs. 'He has an appointment, Wally. Remember our conversation yesterday? About the book? This is Edmund Galloway.'

'Ah yes. The young writer fellow.'

He steps out of the gazebo and, without greeting me, moves over to a wrought-iron table nearby. We sit opposite each other while Penny pours the coffee. In close-up he seems less solid, less overpowering than he appears on stage. The large, penetrating, dark-brown eyes, the square, noble forehead are as imposing as ever. But the face is redder and flabbier than I had expected, and the famous jet-black curls are turning grey. I feel a sharp sense of disappointment, as if I have been offered damaged goods. He exudes a sense of melancholy, which quickly vanishes once he begins to talk.

'I'm now on my fourth Lear,' he says. 'The bugger of it is to find some new way of tackling the great part. Unfortunately modern dress is all the rage these days. Poor old William: the indignities he's had to suffer from these blasted young directors, so desperate to be in the latest fashion!' He seems to notice me for the first time. 'Have you had the pleasure of seeing any of my Lears?' he asks.

I'm prepared for this question. I'd re-read the reviews, and rehearsed a few well-rounded opinions about his performances, none of which I had actually seen. But now the moment has come I grope for my lines. 'Oh no – I mean yes, I did see your third Lear, at the King's. It was... I thought it' (Oh God, what were those adjectives?) 'truly majestic... superb... and wonderfully poignant at the end. And...' I tail off, and feel myself redden.

But Herrick seems unaware of my confusion. 'Ah, that was one of my finest hours. We had some glorious costumes, and I finally had the beating of that wretched storm. Always difficult to make oneself heard above that infernal racket, you know. But I got its measure in the end. Shame about my Goneril, though: too damn nice to boot her father out of doors with any conviction. Rehearsals were a nightmare, I can tell you. The bloody woman kept bursting into tears.'

Penny interjects. 'Come on, Wally, I expect you drove her to it in your usual hectoring fashion.'

'Nonsense, darling. I just told her where she was going wrong. No point in pussy-footing around with women like that.' He launches into other memories, seeming to offer them to the nearby flowerbed rather than to me. I wonder how I can bring him round to the reason for my visit. Luckily Penny comes to my rescue.

'For God's sake, Wally, we know all about your glorious past. Just come back to the present for a while, will you?'

Herrick falls silent. His eyelids droop suddenly; the sadness returns to his demeanour. He stands up and moves across to a silver birch tree. Leaning against it, he lights a cigarette, smokes it for a few moments, then strides back towards us. I marvel again at the power of his movement and the flowing walk, which serve to give him such innate majesty on stage.

He sits again and looks squarely at me. 'So you want to write my story, do you?'

'Very much so. I'd consider it an honour,' I reply, just stopping myself from adding 'sir'.

He leans back in his chair and surveys the garden, as if seeking guidance from the flowers and trees. 'Suppose I let you loose on my Life? It's no longer in my control. Look what happened to Charlie Maxton, the poor sod.'

'I agree, that was a truly appalling book. But that's not the kind I want to write.'

'Is that so?'

His tone is scornful. I can see some flattery is required.

'Certainly not,' I reply. 'What interests me is your artistic life, your rich career in the theatre, your supreme talent as an actor. I believe such crucial matters can be written about without the need to pry into a person's private life.'

He eyes me cautiously. 'Fine words, laddie, but how can I be sure you will stick to them?'

'I hoped my book about William Hall would help in that respect.'

He frowns. 'Ah yes. I did dip into that volume. Not badly written, I'll give you that. But William's was hardly an eventful life compared with mine.'

'But that's my point. What fascinated me were his struggles as a musician, his battles to gain acceptance for his radical style of music, both with the critics and the public. And what goes for him as a composer applies equally to your life and work in the theatre.'

Herrick considers this for a moment, then looks wistfully around the garden. 'I shook them back in the old days, didn't I? Showed them what real, full-blooded acting was about. How to hold an audience in thrall. Of course, the critics hated it: they were all taken in by that namby-pamby style so fashionable in London then. But my public couldn't get enough of me.'

He turns to face me again. 'Of course, you're too young to remember any of that.'

'I'm afraid I am. But—'

'So why on earth should I trust you to understand the struggles I had against those nancy boys?'

Sensing all is not lost, I say, 'Obviously I'd also want to gather the memories of some of those in the profession who worked with you at the time.' But this proved to be a bad mistake.

'My God, there'll be none of that!' he thunders. 'I have far too many enemies in the theatre, all the actors and directors who resented my success with the public. I certainly don't want any of them shoving their oar in.'

I hadn't foreseen this problem, which is a troubling one. But I decide to ignore it for now and concentrate on a more positive element: 'Of course I'd want to show you the chapters in draft as I go along,' I tell him.

'That goes without saying!' he replies with a fierceness that startles me. He rises and strides across to the gazebo, which he seems to treat as a kind of safe haven.

I turn enquiringly to Penny, and whisper, 'I'm not at all clear what he actually wants.'

'I don't think he knows himself,' she says. 'To be honest he's been blowing hot and cold on the idea. It's been Lear and nothing but Lear these last few weeks. He's been having a real battle with the young director. And he's having problems remembering his lines. He's never had that before. So you better tread carefully.'

Herrick ambles back to the table but says nothing. I decide to take the plunge. 'I realise you need time to come to a decision. Now that we've met, perhaps you'd prefer it if I came again after you've finished Lear?'

He laughs sardonically. 'That's assuming we ever open. This director laddie, with his ridiculous baseball cap and torn jeans, wants a cockney East End Lear. I am to be a businessman dividing up my chain of clothes shops between my three daughters. Makes the production more accessible, he said. Brings in the television audience. My God, what a pretentious little prick! This is exactly the kind of dreary idea that's fashionable these days. So I kept my mouth shut.'

He turns to Penny. 'Now, darling, we need to go through the heath scene again.'

He rises slowly and, sweeping a hand through his thick hair, complains loudly to the garden: 'Words, words, words!' I take this as my cue to leave, and signal as much to Penny, who nods in agreement. I feel downcast about his attitude to the book. But at least he's not rejected the idea out of hand. As I drive off I resolve to make a further visit once the run of *King Lear* has finished.

*

I catch up with the production towards the end of its short provincial tour. Usually I am too easily influenced by the reviews, so this time I avoid reading them. I also decide to read the play, having realised to my surprise that I have never done so.

I arrive slightly early at the theatre. The foyer is already packed and humming with eager voices. There's an abundance of silver hair and well-weathered faces. It's mainly a female audience – even on a cold Tuesday evening Herrick the former matinee idol still manages to attract the women. I realise some of them might well have seen his Hamlet in their youth.

Although he had told me this was a very modern production, I am still taken aback by the director's concept. The opening scene becomes a party taking place in fifties London in a seedy East End pub. It's a simple set: a bar in one corner, a few tables and chairs scattered about the room, a darts board hanging on a wall. In the corner a juke box is pounding out 'Fings Ain't Wot They Used to Be'.

Wearing a mauve silk suit and two-tone shoes, and surrounded by his fellow directors, 'Boss Lear' is marking his retirement by handing over the running of his company to his three daughters. Goneril and Regan, in low-cut blouses, tight-fitting skirts and high heels, make their well-oiled, dutiful speeches. Cordelia, in her baggy sweater, blue jeans and CND badge, sulkily refuses to join in the praise game.

The production continues in this vein. Goneril and Regan share out the lines of their longer speeches, becoming a kind of modern Greek chorus, a single force of evil rather than two distinctive women. The sub-plot takes place in the offices of Gloucester & Sons. Edmund, sporting a Teddy Boy haircut and winkle-picker shoes, is plotting to buy up a majority of the shares. Edgar, falsely accused by his brother of planning a takeover, escapes the firm's security guards disguised as an office cleaner, and joins a wretched group of homeless people living on a bombsite.

Gloucester's blinding takes place underneath an office desk, with Cornwall using a ballpoint pen to commit the sickening deed. The storm is created by the Fool, a Chaplinesque figure complete with bowler hat and walking stick. To provide the necessary cataracts he empties the contents of a watering can over Lear, who protects himself from the spray with a golfing umbrella.

Herrick's performance is bizarre. His distinctive, aristocratic voice is transformed by a strange accent apparently rooted in the West Country. For the scenes on the heath he wears ragged jeans, a beanie hat, and a T-shirt with the motto 'Help the Homeless' printed on the front. He suggests Lear's madness with a series of clumsy soft-shoe routines. Finally, instead of carrying on the dead Cordelia in his arms, he wheels her in upright on a trolley, as if she were a piece of luggage.

Not surprisingly the effect, even of Lear's death scene, is more comic than tragic. The opening scene in the pub produces a murmur of surprise among the audience. Thereafter they are quiet for a while, evidently stunned by the extraordinary goings-on. But soon they become restless: muttered conversations and muffled laughter break out in parts of the house, most notably when Lear and the blind Gloucester execute a slow waltz together around the heath. There is the occasional boo, and a man calls out, 'Get a life!', prompting Herrick to glare up at the gallery. At the curtain call the sporadic applause mingles with further boos, and someone shouts out, 'Author!' Herrick refrains from taking a solo bow: he looks grim-faced and totally exhausted.

I had planned to go round afterwards and compliment him on his performance, and at the same time raise again the biography idea. But clearly this is now out of the question. Not only that, I fear this fiasco might turn him off the whole idea of the book. I decide to let a few weeks go by before making another appointment, in the hope he will have regained some equilibrium by then.

*

But after a couple of weeks I get a surprise call from Penny. She sounds desperate.

'This may seem an odd request,' she says, 'but I wonder if you might come down and listen to Wallace talk about the theatre? He's very low after finishing with *King Lear* and reading all those terrible notices. He's going on all the time about what he calls his golden years, to the point of obsession. I just don't have the time to listen to him, and nor do his friends. In any case it needs someone who knows about that era of theatre, as you obviously do. Someone to help him get over the trauma of that dire production. Could you manage this one day soon? You'll be doing him a favour – and me too, for that matter.' As

I hesitate, she adds, 'Of course, it could make him look more sympathetically at the biography idea.'

'I'd need to know pretty soon whether that is a possibility,' I reply.

'I quite take your point,' she says. 'Then you'll come?'

*

I drive down to Hamscombe a few days later. Autumn is starting to tinge the trees copper and gold. In contrast to my apprehensive mood during that first journey, I feel quite eager and hopeful. The balance of power has subtly shifted: I am no longer just the supplicant but potentially a kind of helpmate. In my bag I have an old *Theatre Yearbook* that belonged to my late father, a fellow actor. It contains photographs of Herrick playing Macbeth, which I hope might help to break the ice.

Penny is waiting in the front garden, fiddling with the roses and looking anxious. She tells me Herrick is spending all his time gazing at past production photographs, listening to old recordings, immersing himself in his cutting books, and reading his good reviews out loud.

'His confidence is terribly low,' she says. 'There's no work on the horizon, his agent's not been in touch, and his friends are keeping away. So he could do with a sympathetic listener. By the way, did you see the *Lear* production?'

'I'm afraid I did. It was acutely embarrassing.'

'Well, for God's sake don't mention it.'

As we go into the house, I hear a voice in the distance. Penny shows me into the sitting room where, stretched out on a chaise longue in a purple dressing gown, Herrick is listening to a recording. I slip quietly on to a chair.

It takes me a moment to realise that it's Herrick's voice, speaking Hamlet's 'rogue and peasant slave' soliloquy. I notice how subtly he catches Hamlet's quickly changing mood, from bewilderment – 'What's Hecuba to him or he to Hecuba?' – to fury at his inability to avenge his father's murder. This is not the barnstorming style I expected; it's nuanced, intelligent verse-speaking. I watch him as he listens, his eyes closed, his arms behind his head. His face looks thinner than before, no longer so florid, with more than a hint of vulnerability.

At the end he opens his eyes, notices me, and says, as if we were just continuing a conversation: 'Such fine words… Such poetry… What a craftsman! I think I touched the heights then. My second Hamlet, and my best. Even the critics recognised that: "Herrick holds a mirror up to nature", they said. And they were right.'

He moves across to a drinks tray. 'Time for a sherry,' he says, and before I can reply he is filling two glasses. 'Here's to the divine Will. Where would we poor bloody actors be without him?' He hands me the drink, then embarks on a monologue about the roles he has cherished most, citing Coriolanus, Leontes, Cassius and Macbeth.

I sense my cue. 'I thought you might like to see this,' I say, handing him the *Theatre Yearbook*. 'You might recognise certain pictures in it.'

He takes it over to his desk, sits, and turns the pages slowly, saying nothing. Suddenly he exclaims, 'Oh, it's Rosalind!' He stares at the page for a while, then turns slowly to look out of the window, as if conjuring up the image of his dead wife.

'What a team the two of us made!' he murmurs. 'Her Lady Macbeth was thrilling, and absolutely terrifying. I shall never forget her in the sleep-walking scene. What a splendid actress she was!' He turns back from the window, and I notice his eyes are moist. 'I miss her dreadfully,' he says. 'She was my lodestar.'

'Please keep it,' I say, kicking myself for having failed to notice Lady Macbeth was played by his wife. 'I meant you to have it.'

'I'm grateful,' he mutters, and blows his nose.

Penny comes into the room. 'I'm going to make a light lunch shortly, Mr Galloway. Would you care to join us?'

I look across at Herrick. 'Why not?' he says abstractedly.

*

Penny serves lunch on a large mahogany table in the dining room. Herrick is noticeably silent. He drinks three glasses of wine but only picks at the salmon and salad. Penny keeps the conversation going, talking about the history of the village and asking me about my life in London. Herrick's head starts to droop, and before long his eyes close. Penny beckons me to leave him, and we move to the sitting room.

'He'll doze for a while,' she says. 'It's become a habit recently. Would you feel able to hang on for a bit, while I dash down to the shops? He'll be more alert later, and then you'll be able to mention the book again. Thanks so much.' She disappears before I can agree.

I wander round the room, looking at the posters and photographs on the walls. The posters all have

Herrick's name in large letters above the title. The plays, apart from Shakespeare's, are mostly by writers long forgotten. I peer closely at the photographs of Herrick in various roles, invariably heavily made up and striking melodramatic poses. I browse along his bookshelves, full of the predictable volumes of theatre history, editions of Shakespeare, and actors' memoirs, but also, more surprisingly, many thrillers and murder stories. On the mantelpiece above the Victorian fireplace, between a couple of silver snuff boxes, I come across a framed photo of his wife, decked out in full Cleopatra headdress and costume.

I pick up one of the early volumes of *Who's Who in the Theatre* from the floor and, sitting in an armchair, start to read the many columns devoted to Herrick. I'm so absorbed in the detail of his career that I fail to notice him standing in the doorway.

'So you're still here?' he says, arching his bushy eyebrows.

'I hope you don't mind,' I reply, rising hastily, suddenly feeling like an intruder.

'I see you're reading the profession's Bible. It's not to be trusted, you know. They left out the Cassius I gave at the Birmingham Rep. And they got my club wrong – it's the Garrick, of course.' He looks out into the garden. 'Where is Penny?'

'She had to go down to the village. She suggested I stay on for a little while.'

'To what purpose?' he replies, moving across once more to his desk.

I decide to face the question head on. 'She thought we

might talk further about my writing about your life in the theatre.'

'Oh, there's no chance of that, young man. I've decided to write it myself. How else can the real truth be told?'

I take a moment to absorb this startling news.

'Just take a look around,' he says, gesturing at the walls. 'It's all here in this room, all the material I need to tell my story. And in my head, of course. The memory is as good as ever, the old grey matter still works. So all I'll need eventually is a typist.'

I am lost for words, and my astonishment increases when he adds, 'Do you type?'

I feel a growing anger at his insensitivity. 'I'm a writer, not a secretary,' I tell him. 'And if I may say so, I think you're making a serious mistake in taking this on yourself. Actors' memoirs are notoriously unreliable.'

'Perhaps so when they are written by those with ordinary talent,' he replies calmly. 'I myself don't fall into that category, as my long and successful career makes plain. In my day I was at the very top of my profession.'

Suddenly I no longer want to be in the same room as this appallingly self-regarding man. I tell him I must be on my way and move to make my escape. He makes no effort to stop me. 'As you wish,' he says.

As I climb into my car I notice him standing in the doorway. Clouds have gathered and cast the house into shadow. It no longer looks like the place of promise it had seemed to me just a few hours earlier.

*

This experience had a profound effect on me, and quite turned me off anything to do with the theatre. I reverted to my earlier passion for music, both in my work and my leisure time. I wrote articles and reviews for music magazines, and attended concerts and operas.

I had quite forgotten about Herrick when, some two years later, an actor friend rang to tell me he had died the day before, from a stroke. Apparently he had been found lying in the gazebo, clutching a copy of *The Tempest*. I read the obituaries, which give due credit to his achievement and popularity at the pinnacle of his career, but are scathing about his overblown, old-fashioned style of 'star' acting. They also highlight the number of enemies he had made within the profession because of his monstrous egotism, his jealousies, and, not least, his rampant homophobia. Alas, poor Herrick.

A few days later I saw a brief reference in the press to his funeral, attended by a pitifully small group of elderly actors. Shortly afterwards, as I was writing up a concert review, I received a letter from a firm of Sussex solicitors. In his will Herrick had left me a very modest sum of money, on condition I write his biography, and complete it within two years of his death.

I dropped the letter into the wastepaper basket and turned back to my review.

A Brief Encounter

To Jessica Hall it seemed an age since she had been to Stratford. As she drove across the Warwickshire countryside, memories of that distant occasion came tumbling back into her mind.

What a blissful climax that week had been to her final year at school! She and the other students had camped in a field opposite the Shakespeare Memorial Theatre. They had swum in the Avon with actors in the company, attended stimulating lectures at a Shakespeare summer school, and seen three productions from up in the gallery. It was absolute bliss.

Soon after that idyllic summer her life as a young mother had grabbed her by the throat and never let go. Her son and two daughters had occupied her totally in their childhood. Their large Edwardian house in Evesham had become a bustling crossroads for their shifting friendships, rivalries, quarrels, and sleepovers. But as teenagers they had gradually pulled away from her, and eventually left home. Her daughters had married and gone abroad, while her son, for reasons she still failed to understand, had turned against her.

Now approaching fifty, Jessica had compensated for their loss by immersing herself in charity work. Her husband Max, a wiry, anxious and deeply selfish man, worked for an environmental pressure group. Hiding behind a flurry of policy papers and meetings, he had soon opted out of any domestic responsibilities. Jessica resented his withdrawal, and there had been many rows.

She saw his behaviour this weekend as all too typical. Her sister Melanie, hoping to ease the strain on their increasingly unstable marriage, had bought them tickets for a Saturday matinee at Stratford. Max, a reluctant theatregoer, had grudgingly agreed to the idea, only to back out at the last minute, pleading a climate crisis meeting in Birmingham. Jessica was furious and accused him again of being obsessed with his work.

To her relief, by the time she awoke in the morning he had already left. She decided to go to Stratford anyway. She put on a beige silk blouse and a green cotton skirt, clothes she realised she had not worn for many years. Breakfast alone was a welcome moment of calm: instead of the news bulletins and the *Today* programme, which Max insisted he needed to hear for his work, the purity of a Bach prelude soothed her mind. Once on the road she took in the gentle beauty of the landscape and its succession of pretty villages. She passed a sign announcing 'Welcome to Shakespeare Country', and instinctively tooted her horn.

*

Lennie Jones had come late to Shakespeare. At his Birmingham comprehensive his English class had studied *Julius Caesar* by reading it round the class. This tedious experience had quite turned him off both poetry and drama. A friendly, sensitive boy, he had found an outlet in music and sport, especially football, for which he quickly displayed a talent. He had joined the local youth club, which ran weekly five-a-side games.

One evening the football was cancelled because the roof above the sports room was leaking. Disappointed, Lennie wondered what else was on offer. He decided to try the music room, where there was sometimes an impromptu jam session. But on reaching it he heard no music. Instead, pinned to the door, he found a handwritten notice, stating 'This is the Forest of Arden'. Curious, he entered. He seemed to have stumbled upon a keep-fit class. A group of students were going through a strenuous exercise under the guidance of a man in a grey tracksuit. He saw Lennie and beckoned to him, inviting him to take part. After hesitating for a moment, he thought, 'Why not? It's exercise.' He moved over to the group and joined them.

After a few minutes' more exercise, the man said, 'OK guys, back to the forest. Let's go from "Now my co-mates and brothers in exile".' He approached Lennie. 'Hi there, I'm Fergus,' he said. 'We could do with another lord for this scene. Do please join us.'

'What's this all about?' Lennie said.

'Just a rehearsal,' Fergus replied. 'We're putting on *As You Like It* at the end of term.'

Lennie frowned. 'Oh, Shakespeare.'

Fergus smiled. 'Don't worry, it's not a speaking part. Just sit with those lads and lassies over there, and follow them.'

'No, thanks,' Lennie replied, and started for the door. But as the rehearsal began he stopped and listened...

Hath not old custom made this life so sweet / Than that of painted pomp? Are not these woods / More free from peril than the envious court

...Something in the sound of the words, in the rhythm of the lines, held his attention... *Sweet are the uses of adversity...* He found himself gradually drawn in. At school Shakespeare had seemed like a foreign language; now, suddenly, it had meaning. He became curious about the story... *And this our life, exempt from public haunt, / Finds tongues in trees, books in the running brooks / Sermons in stones, and good in everything...* Hardly aware of what he was doing, he moved over to the group of lords and quietly joined them again.

That evening was a turning point in his life. He stayed with the club's drama group and began to take on small parts in its productions. Soon he moved on to more substantial roles. Acting took over from football as his obsession. It liberated him, took him out of himself, gave him a new confidence. He developed a surprising gift for comedy, and at eighteen applied for and won a place at a drama school for the autumn. He spent the summer stacking shelves in a supermarket and working as a barista in a coffee bar in the evenings.

Then, on an impulse, he decided to go to Stratford, to see *Othello*. He left his tiny bedsit early and hitch-hiked to the outskirts of the city. On arriving at the theatre he was disappointed to find the performance was sold out. He quickly joined the queue for returns.

*

Jessica parked her car and walked briskly through the town centre towards the theatre, passing the many ancient, half-timbered houses. Already the streets were packed with tourists, with more foreign faces and accents than she remembered from her visit as a schoolgirl. As she approached the large red-brick theatre standing by the river she noticed a queue stretching along the wall. With a start she remembered the spare stalls ticket in her purse. She sat down on a bench in the nearby gardens and sized up the queue. She felt uneasy about trying to sell her spare ticket, as if she were some kind of confidence trickster. But she quickly chided herself for being so feeble.

She rose and walked across to the queue. It consisted mostly of couples, who clearly would have no use for a single ticket. A young woman in a vivid floral dress, possibly a student, expressed interest, until she heard the price of the stalls seat. A bearded, middle-aged man seemed a possibility, but he was looking for two seats.

She decided to cut her losses and offer the ticket at half price. She passed several more couples, then reached a tall, dark-skinned young man, wearing jeans and a worn leather jacket, with a knapsack on his back. His initial eagerness turned to disappointment when Jessica told him the cost involved: he confessed he could only afford a gallery seat. She moved reluctantly on, passing more couples, feeling a rising sense of desperation.

Then on an impulse she turned back, found the young man, and offered him her stalls seat at the gallery price. 'Are you sure?' he said.

'I just don't want it to be wasted,' Jessica replied.

'That's really generous of you,' he said.

They detached themselves from the queue and made the exchange.

He then said tentatively, 'Can I perhaps buy you a cup of coffee as a thank-you?'

Jessica had planned to visit Shakespeare's birthplace and his school, then find a restaurant to have lunch. But she had instantly warmed to the young man's manner, and the idea of having company was attractive. 'Yes, I'd like that. I'm Jessica,' she said, proffering her hand.

'Lennie,' he replied, taking it.

*

They found a table in the theatre's café overlooking the river. While Lennie fetched the coffee Jessica gazed across the water, to where she and her school friends had camped all those years ago. She noticed the field where they had pitched their tents was now a car park, and felt a pang of disappointment that such a magic moment of her youth had been obliterated. How did that Joni Mitchell song go? Something about exchanging paradise for a parking lot. She wondered if she had ever been as happy and carefree as she had been that summer.

Over coffee she listened while Lennie talked animatedly. He spoke of his youth-theatre experiences, his hopes for his drama-school course, his desire to make it as an actor professionally. He spoke rapidly, in an attractively musical voice, the midday sun casting an attractive glow on the side of his face. Jessica warmed to his enthusiasm, to the way his brown eyes widened excitedly as he talked about the theatre, and his determination to follow his star.

Suddenly he broke off. 'I'm so sorry. I'm doing all the talking. It's very rude of me. It's not my usual way…' and he trailed off.

'No, I'm really interested,' Jessica said. 'Another coffee? It's my turn.' Her tourist plan had been quietly abandoned.

*

Lennie normally steered well clear of contact with older women. His experience of them had always been negative. One of the worst had been his maths teacher at school. A large, bad-tempered Irish woman, she had constantly berated him for his failure to understand algebra. But the fundamental cause of his aversion was his mother. Her domineering personality, her regular outbursts of fury, and her snobbish criticism of what she called his 'rough' friends, had all blighted his home life and left him deeply resentful of her.

Yet how differently he felt now, talking easily with this friendly middle-aged woman. He realised her generosity over the ticket had helped, as did the sandwiches and fruit she now thoughtfully brought back with the coffee. But he was surprised how quickly he relaxed in her presence, how much he liked listening to her warm, gentle voice. As she told him about her first visit to Stratford he took in her features, and her kindly dark-blue eyes, framed by wrinkles beneath her chestnut-coloured hair.

'I remember seeing an exciting production of *Coriolanus*,' she recalled, 'and a merry *Twelfth Night*. But it was *Hamlet* that was the most thrilling. It was so moving, I was in tears by the end. And the soliloquies were so beautifully spoken.'

'It sounds wonderful,' Lennie said. 'I'm dead jealous. Actually, to be honest, I'm way behind with Shakespeare. I've only managed to see two of his plays, and I've never seen *Othello*. Pathetic, isn't it? I badly need to catch up before term begins.'

*

With time to spare before the performance, Jessica suggested they visit Holy Trinity church, where she remembered Shakespeare was buried. Lennie knew little about Shakespeare's life and happily agreed. Under a cloudless sky they wandered along the narrow lane, past The Dirty Duck, the famous actors' pub. The heat from the sun bounced off the red-brick walls of the old houses, warming Jessica's fair skin, and inducing in her a growing feeling of goodwill.

Why, she wondered, am I so thoroughly at ease with this attractive boy? How very different it is from my broken relationship with my son. She recalled again her Danny's obsessive concern with money and status, his sudden cold demeanour that had led to their estrangement. If only, she thought, I could have connected with him as I am doing now with this modest young man. How dearly I would have liked to have had a son like him. As if reading her thoughts, Lennie asked her about her family and her work. As they walked along Jessica gave him a snapshot of both, omitting the more negative aspects.

They passed along the tree-lined path leading up to the church and entered just as a group of chattering schoolchildren emerged. Inside a handful of tourists were scattered around the church. Several were gathered by Shakespeare's tombstone, where a man was reading the epitaph aloud to a young girl by his side:

> *Good friend for Jesus's sake forbeare, To dig the dust enclosed here.*
> *Blessed be the man that spares these stones, And cursed be he that moves my bones.*

They moved on. Jessica was surprised and shocked when they came across a memorial monument, a coloured statue of Shakespeare sporting a curly moustache and a goatee beard, holding a quill pen and paper, and gazing for inspiration into the distance.

'What a hideous creation!' she whispered to Lennie. 'Shakespeare must be turning in his grave.'

Lennie said, 'He looks more like one of the three musketeers.'

Jessica laughed in agreement.

*

From the moment the play started Lennie was riveted. Transported to Venice, he quite forgot he was in a theatre.

As Iago began to poison Othello's mind, he followed every twist and turn of his evil plotting with rapt fascination. He was surprised at how easily Othello was persuaded of Desdemona's infidelity, and the speed with which he became bent on revenge. Moved by Desdemona's rendering of the Willow Song, he found the last act, as Othello killed first Desdemona and then himself, almost impossible to watch. Throughout he was captivated by the power and music of the words.

Jessica had seen other productions so was less absorbed by the story than by the acting. She was thoroughly convinced by this Iago's evil nature and his skill in concealing it from everyone around him. She was not so impressed by the Othello, who spoke the verse beautifully, but seemed short on the basic nobility the part demanded. She felt the Desdemona caught well the character's innocence and her passionate love for Othello, while Emilia's bawdy nature but basic loyalty was convincing. She appreciated the simplicity of the direction, pleased that the actors were allowed to tell the story without any distracting concept.

*

After the play finished, and they emerged from the theatre with the rest of the audience, Lennie was in a dream. He moved ahead of Jessica and sat on a bench in the nearby gardens, lost in thought. She joined him, taking care not to break the spell. Then a car backfired, startling Lennie back to reality.

He turned to Jessica. 'I really can't thank you enough,' he said. 'I wouldn't have missed this afternoon for anything.'

Jessica touched his arm gently. 'I'm so glad. It was a good production, wasn't it?'

'Oh yes! But I don't think I can put into words what I feel about it.'

'You don't have to. I'm just so glad you enjoyed it.'

They sat peacefully in silence in the late afternoon sun, watching a pair of swans moving elegantly along the glistening river. Neither of them was in a hurry to leave. Eventually Jessica said, 'Perhaps you should come here in the spring? I see from the programme that *Much Ado* is on later in the season.'

'Oh yes, I'd love to do that,' Lennie enthused. 'But I'll have to save up for a good seat this time. You've spoiled me.'

Jessica felt a rush of tenderness towards him. She opened her handbag and handed him a card. 'If you decide to come again, just get in touch with me, and maybe we could go together?'

'Really? Do you mean that?'

'I certainly do.'

Lennie smiled and put the card in his knapsack. 'It's a deal.' He looked at the gathering clouds across the river. 'I guess I should be getting home.'

As they shook hands, Jessica resisted an urge to give him a hug.

*

Over the next few weeks Lennie read three Shakespeare comedies, including *Much Ado About Nothing*. Every week he set aside part of his meagre wages to save up for another Stratford trip. But then the drama-school term began, and totally absorbed his attention. He plunged enthusiastically into every aspect of the course and was soon recognised as one of the more talented actors in his year. When it came to the public showing at the end of term, he was given the chance to share the role of Othello with another black student.

This reminded him of his magical day at Stratford. He wrote Jessica a letter, telling her how proud he was to be playing Othello, suggesting he might now be able to visit Stratford in the spring, and asking her if she still wanted to go with him. But after finishing the letter he couldn't find her card. Only then did he realise how much he was looking forward to seeing her again.

But over the following weeks he became preoccupied with rehearsing *Othello*. He thought of Jessica from time to time, but in the months that followed her bright image gradually faded from his mind.

*

The day after her return home Jessica had phoned Melanie to thank her for the tickets. She told her sister she had managed to get rid of the spare one but made no mention of Lennie. Afterwards she wondered about this omission. Surely there was nothing to be ashamed of or feel guilty about over their time together, was there? A touch of maternal feelings, perhaps, but nothing more, surely? But she found it hard to dislodge Lennie from her mind, and the strong hope that he would manage another visit.

Yet as the weeks passed and spring came and went, she had a feeling that she wouldn't hear from him again. This upset her; it had been such a refreshing moment, one which had briefly illuminated her mundane life. Then she told herself to face facts: it was simply a random meeting, a pleasing interlude, and she should leave it at that. Why, she thought, would a young lad with everything ahead of him want to spend more time with a wrinkled middle-aged woman like me?

Unmasked

The Chorus are sitting in a circle in the large rehearsal room. They are looking forward to working with masks for this production of a Greek tragedy.

The Director arrives. A burly man with a trim beard and a head held high, he exudes natural authority. He takes a chair next to a table covered with a row of full-face masks. He scrutinises the actors for a moment, then in his deep, measured voice he begins.

'The Greeks knew what they were doing,' he says. 'Wearing a mask enabled their actors to deal with the most intense emotions, and yet still be able to describe them to the audience. In this way they could deal with extreme passions, which would be intolerable if expressed naturally. The point was, the mask had no expressions: it was ambiguous, it could laugh or cry depending on what the wearer was feeling.'

He looks slowly round the circle. 'Forget me, forget your colleagues. This is not a group activity; this is about you.' He takes a mask from the table and holds it up face forward. 'To start with, pick a mask that appeals to you. But approach it with care. You must treat it with discretion, with pride. Give it true respect and you'll find it will pay you back. But if you simply treat it as a prop, it won't work.'

He points to the large mirror covering one whole wall of the rehearsal room. 'Look at your face and the mask side by side in the mirror, then put on the mask. Use this moment to become whatever character you see there. Let it take over, then find out how you walk, talk, think, feel. The mask will enable you to change your age, your bearing, your physique, even your gender.'

He puts the mask back on the table. 'The mask will then allow you to reveal aspects of your personality you didn't know existed. It has to be comfortable for you; it has to make you feel free. If you find a mask that gives you a charge, you can add pieces of clothing from the rail over there, or one of the props from the table. But if you feel untrue wearing it, if you feel tense or unhappy, take it off immediately. The masks are not dangerous, but if I tell you to remove it, you must do so at once.'

The actors each take a mask from the table. Several try on two or three before accepting one they are happy with. Each actor works differently: some make use of the mirror, others move around the room in a world of their own. One simply stands still; another struts around in a military fashion; a third tries out different gestures in front of the mirror. A few take an item from the rail: a scarf, a jacket, an overcoat. Gender proves impossible to pin down. Almost everyone moves in slow motion, as if involved in a ritual. No one speaks.

*

Martin is the new newest member of the Chorus, a last-minute recruit. An anxious young man, he is the last to choose a mask. He holds it uneasily, staring into its empty eye sockets, feeling its firm texture. Then, very slowly, he puts it on, and waits.

'I feel as if I'm trapped,' he tells himself after a while. 'I think the mask dislikes me. Yes, I can feel its hostility; it's spreading through me. Oh God, it's stifling. I must choose another.' He does so, and returns to the mirror. 'Ah, now I can breathe properly. This feels much more comfortable.' He pauses. 'And yet it's still not right. It's making me feel sad. I feel like I'm going to cry. I must try another.' After putting on a fresh mask he walks briskly round the room. 'Yes, this one's much better. It's giving me a great burst of energy. This is good: I feel much more relaxed.'

He returns to face the mirror. 'Who is this I'm looking at? It's me, and yet it's not me. I look older and taller; I'm holding my head higher. Suppose I try moving my arms around? How strange, it feels as if I am addressing an audience. Should I speak? No, not yet. I think I need a hat.' He crosses to the rail and selects a brown trilby hat. 'That feels good. Now I'm more secure. It's a mask that likes me. It approves of me.'

*

The Director asks the actors to stop and carefully remove their masks. 'That was a very useful first session,' he tells them. 'I saw some excellent work there. Your level of concentration was impressive. One or two of you even achieved a oneness between mask and body. Some of you perhaps relied too much on the mirror as a safety net. But don't worry, this is just the beginning of the process.'

He invites the actors to share any worries or tensions they have.

One woman says, 'I got a headache trying to mould the mask to my face.'

A man remarks, 'My heart was beating fast, but I had a feeling of great power.'

A second woman explains, 'I was anxious beforehand, but once I put the mask on, I felt liberated.'

Another man confesses, 'I felt a terrible sense of loss. I had to stop immediately.'

Another says, 'When I took the mask off, I felt exhausted, emotionally and physically.'

The Director thanks them for their honest responses. He promises them another session the next day.

*

He begins the second session with a new instruction. 'This time I would like you to become social beings. I want you to engage with another person in the room. But I want you to do this without using your voice. Let your body language be the means by which you convey what you're thinking and feeling.'

The actors select a mask from the table. At first they hold back from approaching one another, preferring to remain isolated, or alone in front of the mirror. But then one woman holds out her hand to another, who hesitates, then takes it. After that many contacts are made.

A man kneels in front of a woman and prays, and she makes the sign of the cross over him. A woman waves farewell, provoking a man to hold his head in his hands. Another man crawls under the mask table and adopts a foetal position. Two men engage in an apparently heated argument. A woman brushes her hair, prompting a man to mime holding up a mirror for her. A couple dance slowly round the room, while a third conducts their music.

*

Martin had been the first to reach the mask table. He wanted to make sure he found the mask he had before, and he had succeeded. He puts it on and looks round the room, wondering who to link up with. But then he becomes agitated.

'My God, what's happening? I don't know who's who anymore. Everyone looks the same. I don't seem able to move. Or even want to. What's stopping me? I had so much energy yesterday. Now it's all gone. Is there something wrong with me? It's not my fault, surely? No, the mask must be to blame. But why? I've treated it so well, I've been respectful. Now I'm completely lost.'

*

That evening Martin sits in the single battered armchair in his untidy flat. He is wearing the same mask, which he has secretly removed from the rehearsal room. His feeling of wellbeing has gone. The old anxiety and insecurity have returned, together with a growing sense of frustration. He grips the sides of the mask hard.

'You were the one I felt at ease with. Now see what you've done. I should have known you would betray me. You're just like all the others after all.' He gets up from the chair, wrenches the mask off, places it firmly on the mantelpiece, and stands squarely in front of it. 'You led me on, didn't you? On purpose. You raised my hopes, then let me down. And now you're mocking me. But don't think I haven't noticed. I can see it in those empty black eyes of yours. But you won't get away with it. Just you wait.'

*

The Director starts the next session by praising the actors. 'You're developing a good understanding of what the mask can do for you. Your imaginations are beginning to take wing, and I'm seeing a lot of fascinating work. So today I want you to engage with each other again but add an extra element: your voice. And this time take a different mask.'

Once their masks are on, the actors begin to speak with each other, at first tentatively but then with growing confidence. Soon the room is buzzing with conversation. Relationships gradually develop, different emotions come into play.

Martin has smuggled his borrowed mask into the room. Surreptitiously he puts it on, then walks across to the mirror, now unoccupied. Once there he starts to address his image in a low voice.

'So here we are again. You thought you'd get away with it, didn't you? You're wrong there. You think you're so smart. But I've found you out. This is me you're dealing with now. Get it? I have the power, I'm the one in charge.' He moves forward to within touching distance of the mirror, his voice steadily increasing in volume. 'How ugly you are. Ugly as hell. Not one redeeming feature. In fact, no features at all. You don't exist. You're a complete nothing without me. And I'll prove it.' He slams his fist against the glass, causing it to crack and shatter his image.

The other actors stop talking and stare across at him. Martin turns to face them, his whole body shaking. With trembling hands he removes his mask, hurls it to the floor, and stamps on it again and again. 'Kill! Kill! Kill!' he shouts. Then abruptly he stops. Kneeling down, he picks up the pieces of the mask and hugs them to his chest in silence, as if in mourning. Then he rises and walks across to the Director.

'Don't blame me, blame this creature,' he says, spilling the remains of the mask onto the table. 'He had it coming to him. He betrayed me, and he's paid the price.' He turns back to the other actors. 'Listen to me, all of you. Don't trust anything the masks do. It's a conspiracy; they're ready to take over. Get rid of them before it's too late. This is your last chance. Your final warning.'

He stares belligerently at them. The actors shift uneasily where they stand. The Director comes out from behind his desk to intervene. Martin stares at him, picks up a fresh mask from the table, and shouts in his face, 'You! Tyrant! Mask yourself!' He thrusts the mask into the Director's face and rushes out of the room.

*

The next morning the Chorus are back in the rehearsal room. The Director stands before them and addresses them calmly.

'What happened yesterday has shaken me considerably. It's not the first time I've had a negative reaction to a mask. But it's never been so violent before. I am conscious of my responsibility to protect you, to ensure this doesn't happen again. So for the moment we will work without masks. I regret this deeply. As you know, I believe wearing them offers the most effective way of exploring these superb tragedies. But I think after yesterday the risk is too great. I hope you understand and will respect my decision.'

There are murmurs of assent from some of the Chorus. The Director returns to his desk, removes his leather jacket, places it over the back of his chair, and takes up his script.

'Let's take it from the beginning of act two,' he says.

Freedom First

SHE HAD KNOWN the speech so well yesterday. She had understood its emotional power, and given it the necessary light and shade. Now, as she waited backstage to be called for her audition, she could think only of the upsetting letter. Why today, she asked herself? Just when I need a clear head.

Every morning for the last few weeks, in front of the long mirror in her small attic flat, Susannah Parsons had stared anxiously at her image. 'Should my hair be shorter?' she wondered. 'What about those creeping frown lines around my eyes? Why does my smile look so weak, so forced?' Yet in the days before the audition, she had found a measure of confidence.

'OK, you may be on the small side, but remember how often you've turned this to your advantage? Especially when you've been cast as the wronged wife, or the comic support. There again, people have said your voice is too low, too masculine-sounding. But that's nonsense: it helps you express strength, determination, courage. And that deep note certainly makes people take notice. All right, your eyes are on the small side, but make-up can do wonders to help. No, your main worry is those missing years. You may have your answers ready, but if they press you, it might all come flooding back.'

In the train she had gone over the speech again. She had spoken it out loud as she walked through the county town, oblivious to the odd looks she received. Once inside the crumbling Victorian theatre she had been shown into a drab little room backstage. She sat there alone, rehearsing her speech once more. Then she stopped, put aside the speech, took out the letter from her bag, and read it again:

Dear Susannah, I think I am too young for you. It came to me in a flash last weekend. My behaviour was ridiculous, I know, but afterwards I tried to understand it. I realised again how much separates us. I am still finding my way. Sure, I still love you, but living together would be different. Please understand—

Just then a tall young woman burst noisily into the room. Susannah hastily crammed the letter back into her bag and looked at the new arrival. The effect was startling. A mass of red hair underneath a beret, heavy eyeshadow, crimson lips. A vivid red silk blouse, scarlet trousers, gold shoes. Susannah was suddenly conscious of her own conventional, muted outfit. Her confidence began to evaporate.

'Oh my God, am I too late?' the newcomer said, collapsing on to a chair. 'I'm down for 11.30. Have they called me? Holly Milton.'

'Not yet,' Susannah replied. 'They're behind schedule.'

'Thank Christ for that!' Holly said, removing her beret. 'That bloody train! It stopped for yonks in some godforsaken field, absolutely full of that ghastly yellow stuff, and right in the middle of nowhere! No one told us anything, surprise, surprise. And the bloody buffet ran out of drink. Can you imagine it?'

Kicking off her shoes, she continued without a pause: 'Last year I went into rep straight out of drama school. God, was that season an eye-opener! Rep is supposed to be a brilliant training ground, isn't it? Well, I learned absolutely zilch, acting in such bilge. I couldn't *believe* such plays existed! Are you familiar with *Lend Me Your Husband*? Or that immortal thriller *The Sinister Eye*? What about *Trousers Galore!*? Yet people came, week in, week out. I was staggered.'

Susannah smiled wryly. Holly seemed to notice her properly for the first time. 'Have you worked here before?' she said.

'Not for some time,' Susannah replied. Not, she thought, since those days of bright possibility. When all the acting avenues seemed open and welcoming. When the thrill of being on stage still felt new and exciting. Can that really have been twenty years ago?

'So what sort of stuff were they doing here back in the day?' Holly asked.

'A couple of Rattigans, a Priestley, *Charley's Aunt*, of course, a thriller or two. And Shaw's *Candida*.'

'You lucky thing. I expect you played some thrillingly meaty parts?'

'Actually I was only in the first two productions.'

'Oh. Why was that?'

Just then a sleek, sallow-faced young man came in, dressed all in black and holding a clipboard. 'Susannah Parsons? We're ready for you now.' She rose and followed him down the stone steps to the back of the stage, past the familiar table piled with props, the stacks of furniture, the jumble of cables, and that distinctive smell she had never quite managed to identify.

The stage looked smaller than she remembered it. As she crossed to the centre she was conscious of the brittle sound of her shoes on the wooden boards. Putting her bag down on a chair she looked out into the darkened auditorium, aware of the old anxiety creeping back.

A voice called out from the void: 'What have you got for us, Miss Parsons?'

'I thought I'd try Mirandolina's soliloquy in the Goldoni,' she replied into the darkness.

'Ah yes, a good choice,' said the voice. 'A delightful character: so ballsy, don't you think? Incidentally, I must apologise for the set behind you. Not very eighteenth century, I'm afraid.'

Susannah laughed nervously. She drew the speech from her bag and glanced at the opening lines. Her hand was already shaking. How ironic her choice now seemed! Perhaps she should have fallen back on something else, something comic, perhaps? Too late now.

'In your own time,' the voice announced.

She put the speech down on the chair, glanced left

and right into the wings – no one there, thank God – and began. '*Marry* him! That would be the day. The husbands I'd have had if I had married all those who wanted to marry *me*!' She staggered on, aware of the shrillness of her voice, conscious that she was rushing the words but feeling unable to slow down. All too soon she reached the end. 'As for marriage, there's plenty of time for *that*. I want to enjoy my freedom first.'

There was a pause. Then the voice said, 'Thank you, Miss Parsons. Just give us a few moments, will you?'

She waited, trying to ignore a growing feeling of panic. 'All wrong, it was all wrong!' she scolded herself. 'I was nowhere near catching her spirit. Where oh where was all the defiance in those words that once so stirred me? They were my anchor, yet today they just seemed hollow. I've blown it, of course. It's obvious. Why should they take me on, even for just one production, never mind a year?'

The silence continued out front. 'So why am I standing here, exposed, just waiting to be rejected?' she thought. 'What's the bloody point?' Impulsively she snatched up her bag, ran into the wings, back through the theatre the way she had come, past a bewildered Holly Milton, out on to the street, and down the hill to the station. On the train she found a seat by the window. Looking out onto the fading afternoon landscape, she saw only a blur. The rhythm of the train mockingly caught that of his words: 'Finding my way… Finding my way.' 'But what about mine?' she thought bitterly.

She left the train and, not wanting to face the solitude of her flat, turned into a coffee shop. Slumped down in a corner with her latte, only dimly aware of the hissing of the coffee machine and the background music, she ran over those moments of panic and dread on stage. 'Never, never, never,' she told herself, 'never will I expose myself again to such an ordeal.'

Gradually she tuned into her surroundings. She began to absorb the detail of the photographs on the walls: the views of Florence and Verona, the bustling street scenes, the families posing self-consciously against whitewashed walls. Her mind drifted back to the sunshine days of her youth, days spent roaming around Italy in carefree style with friends, absorbing the wonderful art, the magnificent old churches and cathedrals, relishing the achingly beautiful language, and indulging in the splendid variety of the food. Not to forget the sublime, unforgettable music – a sample of which now penetrated her consciousness.

She listened, thrilled, as the tenor soared to the climax of a famous aria – which was it? Puccini, surely – but which opera? She bought another coffee and gave herself up to further reminders of her exquisitely unbuttoned past. Now it was Gigli and his passionate rendering of a Neapolitan folk song. Gradually the music started to heal her battered spirit.

She left the cafe reluctantly, the melody still reverberating in her mind as she climbed the stairs to her flat. Once there she found three messages on her answering machine. The first two from friends, wishing her luck with the audition, she hastily deleted. Then she listened to the last message:

> *'Darling Susannah, for God's sake ignore that stupid, utterly selfish letter. I don't know why I wrote it. No,*

I wasn't drunk. I think I just suddenly felt hemmed in, without any reason. I do so much want us to get together. Can you forgive me? I do hope so. You know I love you. Let's do some more flat-hunting at the weekend. Please ring me when you get back, I'll be in the whole evening. All my love, Pete.'

She went across to the attic window with its view across the town's rooftops. She watched the pigeons on the windowsill of the building opposite, moving around restlessly in circles, pairing off, then moving apart again. Suddenly a window opened below them: startled, they rose swiftly into the air and wheeled way over the houses. She watched them until they merged with the hills outside the town.

Moving purposefully back into the room, she picked up her phone, and waited. 'Yes, hello. I want to enquire about flights to Florence... Do you have a seat available this weekend...? Yes, for one... No, just one way... Thank you, that's perfect.'

All is Fortune

Aspiring playwrights are two a penny these days. I'm all too well aware of that. But the steady stream of rejection letters I received was hard to bear. Just occasionally I made some headway. One of my historical plays was granted a workshop in my local theatre. Nothing came of it. Another had a rehearsed reading there. Ruined by poor casting. To survive I was forced to take on occasional painting and decorating work with an actor friend. Result: less time for writing. That lowered my morale further. How much longer could I endure this barren existence?

Then one day I was in the library, reading the theatre reviews and job ads in the *Stage*. I noticed one intriguing ad: 'Warden wanted for West Country cottage museum. Interest in theatre essential. Phone for details.' I don't know why, but as I read these words I felt a churning in my stomach. I rushed out of the library and rang the number on my mobile. A woman answered, rather languidly, I thought. She took my address and promised to send me the details 'when I next go to the post office'.

More than a week passed without a response. I was unable to concentrate; I seemed to have lost all my energy. Why was this silence having such a lowering effect on me? But then a letter arrived with a West Country postmark. I tore it open and read it.

'My late husband's great-grandfather Henry Morrison was a playwright in the Victorian era. His plays were staged by a small touring company but were poorly received and made him little money. To eke out a living he worked as a stage manager for other companies; he once became involved in one of Dickens' home-grown productions.

'On his death last year my husband Ralph Morrison left me a collection of memorabilia relating to Henry's work in the theatre. He wished it to form the basis of a small family museum dedicated to his memory. It was to be situated in the cottage in the grounds of our house. I am now respecting his wishes by setting up such a museum.

'The job of part-time warden will entail sorting out the collection, creating an exhibition, and explaining to visitors Henry's life and career. Accommodation will be provided in the cottage. The initial contract will be for six months. If you are interested ring the number at the top of this letter for an appointment.'

The letter was written on mauve notepaper, headed 'Mrs Jocelyn Morrison, The Lodge, Upper Merryford, Glos.', alongside a crest illustrating a falcon. I knew I was poorly qualified to do the job, but I was desperate.

I phoned and arranged with Mrs Morrison to visit The Lodge the following week.

*

From her voice I imagined an amiable, eccentric old aristocrat gone to seed, rattling around a ramshackle country house in faded, well-worn clothes. But she was nothing of the sort. Sturdily middle-aged, neatly dressed in a green cashmere sweater and brown slacks, her strong-featured face burnt by the sun, she exuded determination and purpose.

'Take a seat,' she said brusquely, showing me into her sitting room. 'I'll come straight to the point. My husband Ralph was under pressure from the family to sell the memorabilia. I tried to persuade him to do so – we needed the money. But he was obsessed with the past and couldn't bear to part with the collection. He thought it was a rich one, that threw a fascinating light on the period, etc., etc.' She spoke in a disconcertingly harsh voice, with a slight trace of a Midlands accent. I became aware of her large hands, which she used vigorously to emphasise her points.

'During his last illness,' she continued, 'he came up with this museum idea, insisting I create it here and open it to the public. He made me promise to carry out this last wish. Frankly I have better things to do, which is why I'm looking for someone to take this blessed thing off my hands.'

I was taken aback by her resentment at having to follow her husband's wishes. Fixing her small, black eyes intently on me, she continued: 'Tell me, why should I give you the job?'

I told her I was a playwright, which I thought might be a good start. 'Oh? So why have I never heard of you?' she enquired. This abrupt question annoyed me. I told her of my struggles to get my historical plays put on. Of my frustration at the failure of many theatres to even respond to my scripts. Of my irritation at receiving merely a standard rejection letter in reply. Of my conviction that my plays were rarely actually read, and when one actually was, I was offered two completely opposing opinions about it.

It was a relief to unburden myself, but I realised my complaints sounded negative. So I ended by telling her I was looking for a fresh challenge.

She frowned. 'You say you're a Londoner. So how would you manage living in the country?'

'Quite easily,' I replied. 'I'm sick and tired of city life, all the noise, the pollution, the traffic, the crowds.'

'You realise I need someone who can work independently once I've shown them the ropes?'

'That's how I like it,' I said. 'To be honest I'm not much of a team player.'

She stared at me for what seemed an age. 'I'm not someone to beat about the bush,' she said finally. 'I've only had two other replies, from two quite obviously unsuitable young women. So I'm going to take a risk and offer you the job.'

This was unexpected. To give myself breathing space I asked if I could see the collection before giving an answer. She nodded, rose abruptly, and strode out of the room. She led me across the spacious garden, along a path flanked by shrubbery and neatly tended flowerbeds, to a large cottage. The building's dark stone, cracked here and there beneath a well-worn thatched roof, gave it a gloomy air.

The inside was equally uninviting. The large front room, stretching the length of the building, had bare whitewashed walls and a flagstone floor. The only heat came from an electric fire placed in a large, tiled fireplace. The smaller back room was filled with a pile of furniture, empty display cases, and screens stacked against the walls.

The front room also contained several large wooden packing cases, labelled 'Notebooks', 'Manuscripts', 'Prompt Copies', 'Playbills', 'Accounts', 'Props', 'Letters'. Mrs Morrison sat down on one case and looked around the room. 'It's strange to see Henry's life all packed away like this,' she mused. 'I suppose we all end up in boxes of one kind or another. He endured a lot of struggle and hardship. Now he's quite forgotten.'

I felt suddenly sorry for her. 'Perhaps this project will help to revive interest in his work?' I said, striving to be positive. 'I take it this is the entire collection?'

She seemed not to hear my question. 'It was really Ralph's baby. It's been sitting here since he died, and I still haven't roused myself to look at it.' She stood up. 'Anyway, to business. Your first task is to sort out the material, catalogue it, and arrange a display. The small back room will be your office. Everything that's in there will be moved into this room; Hawkins, my gardener, can give you a hand.'

'That will be a help.'

'I plan to open the museum after Easter, and keep it open during the summer, from Friday to Sunday. We can fix an admission fee nearer the time. You will be on hand to answer any questions the visitors may have.'

I hesitated for a moment, then pointed out that I had no experience of this kind of work.

'That's not crucial,' she said. 'It's all common sense. And you'll have a free hand in mounting the exhibition.' She showed me the upstairs room, reached by a steep, circular staircase. 'We used to let this floor out in the summer, but there's been no one here since Ralph died.' With its low ceiling, and everything apart from the bathroom contained in one room – a bed, a wardrobe, a full-length mirror, a sizeable desk, and an armchair – it felt cramped. Yet I liked its intimate feel: I could picture myself working there on my current play.

We discussed money. It was just about sufficient to survive on. The hours added up to half the week, enough to give me time to write. Perhaps I should have asked to think it over, but I accepted the job on the spot. I was to start the following week.

'It will be a weight off my mind,' Mrs Morrison said, with uncharacteristic warmth. She offered me a lift to the station, though without much enthusiasm. But it was a fine day, and I said I preferred to walk.

As I walked along the lane the hedgerows on both sides were bursting into life. I felt I was doing the same. I would be starting work just as spring arrived. It seemed like a good omen.

*

On my first day I stood in the middle of the packing cases, wondering which of them to investigate first. My initial idea was to find out what Henry Morrison looked like, and to try to get some impression of his character. But there was no case marked 'Pictures', so I delved into the one marked 'Playbills'.

I discovered three of them were advertising works by Henry himself. They added up to a meagre stage history. *The Railway Men* seemed to have been on for a single week in Portsmouth. *The Devonshire Chronicles* toured small halls in the West Country, starting in Tavistock and ending in Totnes. *No Way to Treat a Man* played just three matinees at the Royal Victoria Theatre in London – I remembered this as the original name of the Old Vic. Underneath the playbills I discovered all three works in manuscript form. I set them aside to read once I had examined the other packing cases.

The letters had helpfully been collected into separate bundles, marked 'Managers', 'Writers', 'Family' and 'Miscellaneous'. Annoyingly, many were not dated, but the handwriting was mostly legible. At first glance the contents looked promising. As I started to read them a small sepia photograph fell out of one of the envelopes. On the back was written in sloping handwriting, 'Henry in the Library'.

It showed a man standing in a book-lined room, leaning stiffly against the mantelpiece above the fireplace. Semi-bald, with thin eyebrows, a long, narrow nose and a complacent mouth, he had the air of a prosperous businessman rather than an artist. He was looking into the camera with a scowl, as if he resented being photographed.

I felt intimidated by his steady gaze, as if I had colluded in his image being captured.

The next day Mrs Morrison announced she would be away for a few days. By now I had finished going through the packing cases. Her husband was right: it was a rich collection. The notebooks contained Henry's candid thoughts about the people he met, including his contemptuous views of theatre managers and actors. The prompt copies relating to his work as a stage manager contained valuable glimpses into the staging conventions of the day. There were several account books, in which he had meticulously entered details of his fees, royalties, and the costs of staging a play in different theatres.

At the bottom of one case I had a surprise. Wrapped in a white cloth and tissue paper I found a suit, a waistcoat, and a bow-tie, all in good condition. The dark-blue suit, clearly of good quality, had a green thread woven into the material. Inside the jacket was a label marked 'Marsh & Marsh, Tailors, Belvedere Street'. The waistcoat was a subtle olive-green, the bow-tie dark brown. I decided to ask Mrs Morrison about them on her return. I took them upstairs, hung the suit and waistcoat in the wardrobe alongside my jacket and shirts, and put the bow-tie in a drawer with my socks.

The props packing case contained many items used in productions of different eras. Intriguingly, none of them was labelled, so I compiled an inventory. There were two swords, a gun, a dagger, three fans, a quill pen and inkwell, a bunch of plastic fruit stuck on a plate, a set of goblets, two small lamps, a hammer, a pipe, a paperweight, and an empty picture frame. I pondered how best to display them. I decided to read Henry's plays, to see if I could match the props to them.

After reading them I could see why he had achieved so little success. *The Railway Men* was a ridiculous, ill-written melodrama about a landowner fighting a rearguard battle against the coming of the railways. He was murdered by his ambitious son, who was in league with the railway company. *The Devonshire Chronicles* proved to be a tame, episodic story of three families living in different towns in the county, and their efforts to make a living off the land. And *No Way to Treat a Man* was a farce about marriage, involving three couples. Its leaden dialogue was swamped by extraordinarily convoluted stage directions.

Then I discovered a fourth play. Concealed at the bottom of a different packing case, *All Is Fortune* was strikingly different. It centred on the imagined early life of Shakespeare's Malvolio, before he became a steward in Olivia's household in *Twelfth Night*. It highlighted his struggle to escape his poverty-stricken background and to improve his lot by seeking employment in Illyria. He worked as an inn-keeper's assistant, a junior clerk, and an apprentice baker. But his cold, aloof manner alienated his fellow workers, and he had been sacked from each job.

The play was written with panache and showed strong sympathy for young Malvolio's situation. The dialogue was realistic; the plot, which included a failed love affair, was well constructed. It felt as if it had been written by another playwright entirely. Since there were no playbills publicising it, I assumed it had never been staged. Perhaps Henry had never submitted it to the theatre managers he so obviously despised? I put it in a separate file, deciding to read it again in order to copy out a page or two to put on display.

The following day Hawkins the gardener helped me shift the furniture. He was a friendly, outgoing fellow, in his rough brown shirt and baggy green corduroy trousers. When I complimented him on the beauty of the garden, he explained with obvious pride the improvements he had made. 'The garden was Mr Morrison's territory,' he told me, 'until his illness made him lose interest. Since then she's let me have my head, Mrs Morrison has. She's not interested herself. Never has been really.' He approved of the museum scheme. 'It's good to see the old cottage being used again,' he said, as we worked. 'It badly needs warming up, to have a spot of human contact and tender loving care.'

When Mrs Morrison returned she was grudgingly satisfied with my progress. 'It's coming along,' she said, looming large in the doorway. She surveyed the main room, which looked something like a museum should. The display cases were full of judiciously chosen items, including a few of Henry's letters. I had covered the walls with the Victorian playbills, and panels explaining Henry's life.

'It wasn't a difficult task, it's such a fascinating collection,' I said, treading carefully. Avoiding any mention of the playscripts, I praised the extensive range of playbills, the spirited letters, and the fascinating collection of props.

She made no direct comment but wandered round the room, scrutinising the exhibits carefully. Then suddenly she stopped, turned to me, and said sternly, 'There's too much on the theatre generally, and not enough on Henry himself. He just doesn't come alive. I'm sure Ralph would not be pleased. The few letters you've put out in the cases are of little interest, except for the Dickens connection. And where, for God's sake, are his plays?'

Her comments shook me. They also annoyed me. So much for my freedom to create the displays as I saw fit! In truth, Henry was not a fascinating figure. As for the plays, she had a point, although luckily she didn't ask my opinion of them. I said I would take on board her criticisms, make a few changes, and display some sample pages from the plays.

'Please do so, and do it quickly,' she said. 'Time is now of the essence.' She left, unsmiling. I realised later I had forgotten to mention the clothes I had found.

A few days later, when she went shopping in nearby Castletown, I decided to give myself a day off and explore the surrounding countryside. Preparing to get dressed, I opened my wardrobe, and saw the suit and waistcoat hanging there. I laid them on the bed and tried to imagine their history. Was this a costume worn by a character in one of Henry's plays? Or was it an outfit of his own, which had some special significance for him? I could find no clue to solve this mystery.

The colours of the three items were an odd mixture. I found the green waistcoat especially attractive. I took it over to the window to examine it in a better light. I noticed how well its colour toned in with the leaves of the trees outside. I hesitated, then slipped it on. It felt very snug, and in the mirror it looked smart, even quite modern. I went across to my desk, took out my pencil and writing pad, sat in the chair, and imagined myself sitting for a portrait of 'The Writer in His Attic'.

Since being in the country I had hardly glanced at my play. I had tried to clear my head of the museum work in the evenings but had found that impossible. Now I felt moved to try again. I immediately saw what had been holding me up: a key scene in the first act was in the wrong place; I had placed it too early. I fixed the problem and found the words in the next act starting to come unexpectedly easily. The characters knew what to say without any help from me. Time passed without my noticing it; I only stopped when I felt hungry. I lay down my pencil with a feeling of exhilaration.

I prepared myself a light lunch and mused on the morning's happening. Why had I suddenly found this rare facility to write? Was it because I was coming to the work with a fresh pair of eyes? Or had the waistcoat perhaps acted as a kind of talisman, subconsciously filling me with renewed inspiration? And if so, was this because of its association with another playwright from another time? This seemed a pretty fanciful notion. Yet I had certainly experienced a new kind of creative release, writing non-stop for several hours.

After lunch I decided to take a walk. I put the waistcoat on the back of the chair, seeing it now as part of my writing equipment. I set off to climb to the top of the hill behind the cottage. The sun had wrapped the landscape in a soft afternoon light, displaying in the distance the patchwork of green fields, the ancient oak trees, the fast-flowing river. Immediately below me was the village, with its timbered and stone cottages painted in pink, lemon and white lining the main street. I could see the pond on the village green, graced by a pair of swans. There too was the traditional war memorial, the sturdy Norman church with its medieval tower and a yew tree shading its lychgate, and the thatched village pub, with its hanging baskets and a wagon wheel standing against its creeper-covered wall. All these traditional rural images must have been very familiar to Henry Morrison. They filled me with a desire to know more about his life.

The next day I booked an ad in the *Merryford Courier* to publicise the museum's opening, and was promised some editorial coverage. On publication day I walked down to the village to buy a copy. The ad was in the 'Local Events' section, but it took me a while to find the editorial piece. I finally found it on the appointments page, which was worrying. But worse was to come: under the headline 'Old Writer Honoured', the piece referred to 'Henry Morrissey, the Edwardian poet, whose lost poems are now on display at Merryford Village Hall'.

I was astonished. How was it possible to get so many details wrong? I rushed to the paper's office and demanded to see the editor. A tall, fair-haired young man appeared. He listened with obvious boredom to my angry complaint, then blithely blamed the error on a student doing work experience. He wearily agreed to run a corrected piece next week, and to repeat the ad. At least they would appear in time for the museum's opening.

I felt obliged to tell Mrs Morrison what had happened. I found her in the kitchen preparing her lunch. 'Typical of that wretched publication since the old editor left,' she said. 'I hope you gave them hell.' The corrected piece duly appeared the following week, and we soon had several phone enquiries.

With the exhibition nearly completed, I returned to my play. Seeking inspiration, but feeling a little foolish, I put on the green waistcoat again. This time I struggled in familiar fashion and was unable to focus on the next scene. I took off the waistcoat and went for a walk around the grounds. Sitting on a seat under an old oak tree, a thought occurred to me. Perhaps inspiration would return if I also put on the other items?

I returned to the cottage, opened the wardrobe, and took out the suit and bow-tie. I slipped into the suit, which was slightly tight but not uncomfortable. Having never worn a proper bow-tie, I needed the bathroom mirror in order to put it on. I examined the effect with some pleasure. I moved back to my desk, opened up my script, and set to work. But again it was to no avail. I did get a couple of pages of dialogue down, but they felt unreal, and I quickly discarded them.

I left the clothes on during my lunch break, hoping to try again in the afternoon. Before that I put the finishing touches to the final display case. Then Mrs Morrison walked in.

'Ah, getting into period, I see,' she said, with a hint of scorn in her voice.

'What? Oh yes,' I replied, with a nervous laugh.

'Where did you find the outfit?'

'Oh, in the charity shop,' I heard myself say, adding hastily, 'The one over in Castletown.' After a moment I added, 'I was thinking, if you approve, that I might perhaps wear it for the opening. If that doesn't seem too, well, absurd.'

'I leave that to you,' she replied. 'I don't see why it should be a problem.' A rare smile threatened to cross her face. 'It would certainly add a novel touch.' For once she seemed almost human.

I decided to make a brief speech at the museum's opening. But I needed to do my homework. I spent several hours in the Castletown library, researching the theatre in the Victorian period. Although I was well informed about Henry's career as a playwright, I was ignorant about the conditions in which he struggled to make his name.

I sat in the high-ceilinged, appropriately Victorian building. I discovered that melodrama, full of moral sentiment, was the kind of play favoured at the time by both managements and audiences. *Pure as the Driven Snow, or Tempted in Vain* was a typical example. Spectacle was also much in favour, with Dion Boucicault, a hugely popular writer, its master.

Trains, carriages, pigs, goats all made their appearance on stage during these years. Later there came the domestic plays of someone called Tom Robertson, known as the 'cup-and-saucer' drama. But no major dramatist emerged until Shaw and Ibsen burst on the scene towards the century's end. Clearly Henry was not part of any golden age for playwrights.

I was working on my speech when Mrs Morrison paid me another visit. She didn't look at the exhibition but simply said, 'I've had another thought. Since you have the costume and know all about his work, why don't you actually play the part of Henry tomorrow?'

This notion quite threw me. Acting had never been part of my ambition in the theatre. My first thought was to reject her idea. But she was looking at me in a way which made me feel uneasy. 'That would be a bit of a challenge,' I said. 'Let me think about it.'

'Of course,' she said. 'Let me know in the morning.'

*

The opening of the museum was a failure. Only two dozen people turned up, and a decidedly mixed lot they were. I recognised a handful of folk from the village. Most of them walked briskly round the exhibits and said little. There was a small group of young women, probably students, a couple of whom took notes, which I found gratifying. An older woman made the mistake of bringing along her two noisy young children. They quickly got bored and forced her to leave.

I noticed two middle-aged men, dressed identically in black polo-neck jerseys and jeans, examining the exhibits with particular interest. Also among the small crowd was the manager of the theatre in Castletown, a man with an owl-like face, accompanied by a small, dark-skinned woman. Mrs Morrison had also persuaded a few of her county friends to come. But they seemed less interested in the exhibition than in knocking back the wine and nibbles on offer, and exchanging gossip,

Having reluctantly decided to take up Mrs Morrison's suggestion, I had decked myself out in Henry's suit, waistcoat, and bow-tie. I felt awkward to begin with, standing at the door and greeting the visitors 'in role'. But I soon started to enjoy myself. I gave a brief speech in the guise of Henry, saying how gratified I was that my work should be rediscovered, and to see my life set out in such fascinating detail. I explained I would happily answer any questions people might have.

I fielded half a dozen, about my family (they were originally businesspeople from Edinburgh), what I thought of Dickens (a wonderful talker, always full of energy), what tickets to the theatre cost in my day (I referred the questioner to the handbills on the walls), and whether I ever wrote a novel (I never could find the time). The one question that challenged me came from one of the men in black, who asked about my plays, and wondered why none of them were on display.

'A fair question,' I replied. 'The fact is I struggled for years to get my plays staged, and received many rebuffs and rejections. As you can see from the posters, I did manage to get the occasional booking for three of them. But I found it all very dispiriting. Theatre managers were very conservative and preferred to stick to melodramas rather than anything more realistic. So eventually I sold my manuscripts for a paltry sum to a dealer in theatrical memorabilia.'

I was rather pleased with my improvised response, and especially amused that I should sell off Henry's life's work without a second thought. Unfortunately Mrs Morrison overheard this last remark and tackled me about it afterwards.

'I hadn't realised he sold his manuscripts,' she said. 'That seems surprising.'

'To be honest,' I replied, deciding I would be, 'I made that last bit up. I've read the plays and, frankly, they're not up to much, and the surviving reviews are poor. So I thought it best to omit any reference to them in the exhibition, beyond the posters.'

'And you took this decision without consulting me?'

'I assumed you'd rather they weren't exposed to the public gaze.'

'On the contrary,' she said, 'I think people should be free to make their own judgements as to their quality. In any case, I don't approve of you playing fast and loose with Henry's work. I want you to make a summary of the plays, select a sample page or two from each, and exchange them for items in one of the display cases.'

'Of course, if that's what you want—'

'It is. And I'd like them to be in place by the time we open again next weekend.'

I carried out her wishes, putting together the summaries, copying out two pages from each of the plays staged and, wincing as I did so, putting the new material on display. She dropped in the next day, took a look at them, muttered curtly, 'I suppose that will do,' and left.

But I had started to worry about *All Is Fortune*. It was clear that I was doing Henry an injustice by not at least referring to it in the exhibition. I took it out from my desk drawer and read it again. I marvelled at how accomplished and imaginative it was, how different in every respect from his other plays. Perhaps it was the work of a rival playwright, who had sent it to Henry, who had done nothing with it? And yet the handwriting was clearly Henry's. But perhaps – by now my mind was shifting gears rapidly – it had indeed come from another writer, and Henry had copied it out so as to pass it off as his own. But I quickly dismissed the idea.

*

The attendance at the museum's second weekend opening was again disappointing. After the last visitor had left I returned to work on my play. But I made little progress, even with Henry's waistcoat on. *All Is Fortune* was weighing on my mind. I read it for a third time, envying again its excellent qualities. Why couldn't I write with that kind of confidence and fluency? It was written convincingly in the Elizabethan manner but also felt very modern, a balance I could never strike successfully in my own historical plays.

Then I had an idea. Why didn't I send *All Is Fortune* off to a theatre in the West Country but under a name other than Henry's? I needed to omit the title page which had his name on it, but that was easily done. I felt Henry's shade would approve of my scheme, whether or not he was the play's author.

I dispatched the manuscript to the Monument theatre in Tadchester, well known for its policy of discovering and staging forgotten plays. Using the false name Tom Stapleton, I explained in a covering letter that I was a playwright myself, and that I had found the manuscript in the attic of my house among my great-grandfather's papers, and assumed he had written it. I spelt out why I admired the play, and suggested that, apart from its quality, it would be of historical interest. Knowing how careless theatres can be, I made a couple of copies in the local library before taking it to the post office.

I was intrigued to know how the theatre would react – if they ever did. But to my surprise I received a reply within a week, surely a record time for any theatre. Even more surprising was the contents of the letter from Monument's artistic director Sheila Taylor.

She said her theatre was most intrigued by this interesting work, with its absorbing story and finely drawn characters. Given the use it makes of Malvolio, she continued, they would be keen to discuss the possibility of staging it next year in their 'Beyond the Bard' season. There was, however, a worrying final paragraph: 'Although it will not affect our desire to stage the play, we would welcome confirmation that this is a play by your great-grandfather Thomas Pritchett, since this could have a bearing on the copyright situation.'

This was a complication I hadn't foreseen. How could I prove the provenance of the play when my family papers were a figment of my imagination? I agonised over the options open to me. Finally I spent several hours typing out the play on to my computer, using one of the copies I had made of the original. I then sent a brief confession to Sheila Taylor:

'I'm afraid your instinct was correct. The story about my great-grandfather's papers was an invention: no such papers exist. I must apologise for this mild deception. The play is in fact one of my own, which I copied out by hand from my computer to give it a Victorian feel. I realise this was a mistake, and I apologise. I hope this matter will not affect your decision to stage the play, and I look forward to meeting with you to discuss its production.'

I had, of course, kept my action a secret from Mrs Morrison. But soon afterwards she came into the museum holding a box, a rare smile on her face. 'Hawkins has come across something else, hidden at the back of his toolshed,' she explained. 'Goodness knows how it came to be separated from the rest of the material.'

'What is it?' I asked.

'Another play, called *All Is Fortune*. Attached to it is a note from Ralph, saying that it's a very original work, and that he had made a copy in case the Merryford Players might like to stage it. That was a surprise: Ralph had little time for the local am dram group.'

I felt a sudden urge to lean against a wall.

'Anyway,' she continued, 'make a summary of it, and put some sample pages on display. Please give it priority. I'll contact the am dram people and see if they're interested. It could be good publicity for the museum.' And putting the box on the table she left as suddenly as she had arrived.

During the next three days I found it extraordinarily hard to concentrate on fitting the play into the display. I felt overwhelmed by my double deception. I was horribly trapped, and unable to see what to do next. Then Mrs Morrison came over one Friday afternoon with yet more bad news.

'I've tracked down Viola Mortimer, who runs the Merryford Players. I told her about Henry's play, and she's keen to read it. So please take the manuscript down to her cottage in the high street, having first taken a copy. Tell her I'm away for a few days until next weekend, but that I hope to hear from her soon after that. Here's the address.'

That evening I sat in great agitation in my room, trying to see a way out of my dilemma. In the morning I walked down to the village, having decided simply to deliver the manuscript and leave. But Viola Mortimer insisted I stay for a coffee and discuss the play. A slim, uninspiring woman with a shrill voice and badly dyed hair, she asked me what I thought of it. I said as casually as I could that it was 'of some interest'.

But then came another bombshell. 'Apart from managing the Players,' she added, 'I also do some informal scouting for new plays for professional theatres in our region. So if it's any good I might pass it on to the literary manager at the Monument theatre in Tadchester. Do you think Mrs Morrison would be happy for me to do that?'

I could feel my hand starting to shake. I quickly put my coffee cup down. 'I don't know,' I said, stalling. 'She's a bit unpredictable.' I was now desperate to escape. I stood up. 'She's away now, but I'll talk to her when she's back. Please excuse me, I have to go.'

*

That evening I thought long and hard. How on earth was I to prevent my double dealing getting out? It would certainly mean the end of the museum job. I realised my only hope was to make a second confession to Sheila Taylor, but this time face to face.

I took the train to Tadchester the next day. I had decided to wear Henry's clothes, which I thought might bring me luck for what was bound to be a difficult conversation. I had made a hasty phone call first, just to establish if Sheila Taylor was in the theatre, but I made no appointment – I needed to see her urgently. When I arrived at noon I was told her present meeting would finish shortly. I waited nervously in the foyer.

She soon emerged, an attractive dark-haired woman, stylishly dressed, and much younger than I had expected.

Glancing discreetly at my unusual outfit, she shook my hand warmly. I explained who I was, that I was in town to meet a friend, and wondered if she had a few minutes to talk about *All Is Fortune*.

Her eyes widened in surprise. 'Why, yes, I'd like to discuss it with you,' she replied, adding, apparently without irony, 'Good of you to drop by.' She showed me into her tiny office, and I decided to waste no time in confessing.

'I wanted to apologise for deceiving you,' I said. 'It was not very clever of me, and I shouldn't have done it.'

She smiled. 'I must confess to being rather shocked at first. But then I read the play again, and it still seemed to me an excellent piece of writing. So now we have clarity on the authorship, I'd like to continue to consider it for our "Beyond the Bard" season. We'll be finalising the programme shortly.'

'I'm afraid there's a further complication,' I said, trying not to avoid her eye.

She laughed. 'You mean you've sent it to another theatre! I wouldn't blame you for that.'

'No, no, worse than that,' I said. 'It's actually not my work at all.'

This did startle her. As I told her about Henry Morrison and how I had discovered his play, I was overcome with a great desire to escape from the room. I watched her face: she seemed to be experiencing conflicting emotions. Finally she spoke.

'I suppose I should be angry with you, but actually I'm not. I'll tell you why. I'm impressed by the ingenious way you have handled this deception, and your honesty in confessing to it – twice. It's a quality in short supply these days in the theatre.'

I was flabbergasted, and temporarily speechless.

'Also,' she continued, 'I can see you have a good instinct for what makes a good play. So here's a proposition. It's difficult to find good readers for the many scripts submitted to us. How would you feel about becoming one of them?'

It took me several moments to absorb this unexpected offer. 'Are you serious?' I said finally.

'Certainly. The pay is peanuts, I'm afraid. But I think it would interest you to see what people are writing about. Anyway, have a think about it, and let me know.'

I finally came to my senses. 'I don't need to think about it,' I said. 'I'd simply love to do it.'

She gave me a wide smile that seemed to warm the room. 'Good. In that case let's discuss it over lunch. Nice suit, by the way.'

*

After that day events moved fast. Shortly after our meeting Sheila decided *All Is Fortune* should open the 'Beyond the Bard' season. This delighted Mrs Morrison, especially as the news increased the number of visitors coming to the museum. I didn't tell her the whole story, and she was too pleased to ask me about the details. I worked out my six-month contract with her while taking on a growing number of scripts for Sheila. I found it stimulating work.

In the autumn Sheila offered me a part-time job with a reasonable salary as the theatre's literary manager. We quickly developed an excellent working relationship, as I knew we would. *All Is Fortune* gained excellent notices and eventually transferred to a large regional theatre in the Midlands.

My new job proved all-absorbing, and I found it difficult to find time to write my play. Then one day I realised my long-held desire to be a playwright had completely gone. I felt liberated.

Surviving

I DIDN'T RECOGNISE HER at first. She was sitting alone in the desolate, half-empty beach café, looking out to sea. Although her table was just a few feet from mine, I could see only her profile. But I sensed something familiar. Then she turned in my direction, and I saw it was Gwen Williams.

Twenty years ago we had been at drama school together. I was startled by the change in her appearance. Her hair was now ash-blonde and cut short in tight, neat waves, revealing a small pair of earrings. She wore a well-cut, dark-blue jacket over a white blouse, with a string of pearls at her throat.

This was not the Gwen I remembered as a student, with her dark, luxuriant hair cascading down her back, her heavy black eye make-up, her vivid, quirky clothes. She was merry, impulsive and self-assured, and blessed with an anarchic sense of humour. Famed for her wicked imitations of our teachers' mannerisms, she also shone in comic parts in our student productions; her Mrs Malaprop, I remember, was a triumph.

I was in two minds whether to approach her. I thought further about our relationship in those youthful days. Back then I had been bowled over by her vibrant personality; her warm smile made you feel the sun had just risen. I even believed myself to be in love with her. But she quickly sensed what was going on. 'Let Plato be our guide, darling,' she said, with that glorious throaty laugh of hers. Having little confidence in myself then, I reluctantly agreed.

After that we became close friends. I too was involved with the dramatic society, and we spent a lot of time together, hearing each other's lines, rehearsing scenes, or just hanging out. Yet despite our friendship I was never clear about her background. She claimed to be Welsh, as her name suggested, but her vowels had a distinctly northern sound. Sometimes she hinted at an aristocratic background, at other times a lonely childhood in a country cottage. I never managed to resolve this enigma.

So what was she doing in this bleak, rundown seaside town? Suddenly I felt compelled to find out. Picking up my cup of coffee I walked across to her table.

'May I?' I said, indicating the empty chair opposite her.

'Help yourself,' she said, looking up briefly, before returning to the book she was reading. Her blue-green eyes seemed smaller than I remembered, her face noticeably thinner, her skin less smooth. I felt sad to find her so changed. I waited for a while, but she remained deep in her book.

'It's been a long time, Gwen,' I said eventually.

She looked up, puzzled for a moment; then recognition slowly came. 'Charlie?' she said warily.

'That's me,' I replied.

She laid her book aside and sat back in her chair. 'Whatever brings you to a place like this?'

I tried to keep my tone light. 'To see if the coffee has improved since last year.'

She frowned. 'No, you know what I mean.'

I explained that I came here every summer to stay with my sister. Working all hours running a London fringe theatre, I badly needed to escape the relentless pace of city life and the intense demands of my work. I wanted to enjoy the soothing calm of the countryside and do some serious walking.

She nodded but made no comment. Her silence became uncomfortable.

'And how about you?' I said, trying to keep the conversation going. 'What are you up to these days?'

'Surviving,' she said, gazing out at the windswept beach, where only a handful of people were strolling about. I waited for more detail, but none came.

'In the profession, I hope,' I said eventually.

She sighed. 'Yes, if you can call it that. I've thought time and time again of giving it all up.'

'Seriously? I'm very sorry to hear that.'

Her voice suddenly rose in anger. 'God, Charlie, really, what's the point of it all? The uncertainty, the stress, the constant rejection? It's just not the kind of life I hoped for. I mean, I spend days and days waiting for my phone to ring, feeling absolutely wretched.' She lifted a pale hand to her forehead. 'I'm ashamed to admit it, but most of the time I just don't feel like going out. Auditions have become sheer hell: the more of them I fail, the more desperate I become. I just thank my lucky stars for the odd voice-over. I hate doing them, I disgust myself, it's so demeaning; but they're my only lifeline.' She lowered her voice again. 'I lie awake for hours at night, thinking how all these years spent pretending to be someone else have been such a waste of time. A complete bloody waste.'

I was struck by her profound despair. Where was that overflowing vitality, that eager optimism she showed in those distant days of hope and gaiety? I felt a rush of pity for her, and a need to lighten her gloom.

'It's certainly a tough life,' I said. 'But you've done pretty well to keep going. Unlike so many others from our time.'

There was another silence.

'So are you working now?' I ventured.

'For once, yes, as it happens,' she said. 'A short tour. Just a few village halls and arts centres around the county. We end here on Saturday. After that, who knows? I have absolutely nothing lined up.'

'So you're playing *here*? What's the show?'

'Oh, the usual third-rate nonsense. A ridiculous story about a scandal in a vicarage in a Welsh village. It's written by the director, a truly ghastly little man. I only have a small part, but I suppose it's better than nothing. Just about, anyway.'

'I must come and see it,' I said impulsively.

'Oh no, please don't do that, Charlie,' she replied quickly. 'You'll hate it.'

I insisted, I suppose through an instinctive loyalty to

our shared past. 'We'll have a drink at the bar afterwards,' I said, adding, 'for old times' sake.'

Gwen shrugged and drained her coffee. 'All right, but don't say I didn't warn you. Now I must go and psych myself up for the matinee. We'll get the usual half-empty house, so you'd do better to come tonight.'

We walked along the seafront to the theatre. Small waves rippled gently onto the beach, and a slight breeze caught Gwen's hair. She said nothing about her personal life, and I felt it best not to enquire; I had noticed she wore no ring. We talked of friends at drama school, of the lucky few who had made their mark, of the many others who had fallen away or fled the profession in search of security.

At first she seemed uneasy recalling the old days. But as we talked I caught the odd glimpse of her youthful spirit breaking through. At one moment she stopped and gazed intently out to the horizon. 'My father was once in the navy,' she said, her voice momentarily bright. 'He went everywhere.' I waited in vain for more details.

At the far end of the front we reached the little theatre. It was a ramshackle, single-storey building, covered with a row of forlorn miniature flags. I wished her good luck as she went round to the stage door. In the foyer I bought a ticket for the evening performance. On the walls hung framed posters of past productions and signed portraits of West End stars who had played here on their way to better things. Back outside I examined a glass case containing photos of the cast of the current show. There was Gwen in a carefully lit photo, clearly taken many years ago.

To fill the time before the show I had a leisurely pub lunch, browsed in the local second-hand bookshop, and then took a long walk along the cliff above the town. I was uncertain whether to return to the theatre. Did I really need to undergo a potentially depressing evening? In my constant search for promising new writers I'd had quite enough of such bleak occasions back in London. In the end I felt I couldn't let Gwen down.

The play, set in the village vicarage, was indeed terrible beyond belief: the dialogue was trite, the story absurd, the characters mere stereotypes. The set was tawdry, most of the acting was unbelievably poor, and the direction was virtually non-existent. But the evening was saved for me through one speech by Gwen.

As the downtrodden wife of the vicar, her part mostly involved providing drinks and cups of tea, and acting as a feed to the principal characters. But in the last act she had a telling little speech: she spoke about the barrenness of her existence, the hopes she once had of something different and far richer. Here, in an evening shot through with unreality, she conveyed genuine suffering, all the more poignant for being put over in an understated way. It was a moment out of kilter with the rest of the evening, and it held me spellbound.

Afterwards I waited at the bar for Gwen to appear. Over a whiskey I thought more coolly about her speech. It had astonished me to see someone I remembered as a skilful young comic actress hinting at tragedy with such unerring skill. Clearly, in portraying the wife's disillusion so convincingly, she had drawn deeply on her own despair. I looked forward to praising her for it.

The actors began appearing in the foyer, milling around and noisily greeting their friends. There was no sign of Gwen. Then one of the actresses approached me, asked if I was Charlie, then handed me a note. Its contents took me aback:

Charlie – I'm truly sorry to stand you up, but I think it's best if we don't meet again. Digging up the past has been too painful. It reminds me how thoroughly I've wasted any talent I might have. This feeling simply overwhelmed me tonight. As I'm sure you noticed, I struggled desperately to make anything of my one decent speech. Please believe me, my work hasn't always been so dreadful. But tonight I hit rock bottom. So it's time to face facts and give up this ridiculous charade. Please don't think too badly of me, old friend – Gwen.

I walked back along the seafront to my car. A sharp wind had risen. Under a full moon the waves were tumbling fiercely onto the pebbled beach. I drove back to my sister's house through the dark country lanes. I reflected on the desperate cruelty of theatrical life, on the broken dreams of the thousands who had started out hoping fervently for success, only to find it all too soon become a distant dream.

Dateline Moscow

... While we've been on air reports are coming in about an incident in Russia. Michael Creasy, our Moscow correspondent, is outside the city's main theatre this lunch time. What can you tell us, Michael?

It's a pretty complex and confusing story, Bridget. I'm standing outside the famous Moscow Art Theatre on a freezing cold day, with Theatre Square covered in several feet of snow. According to a source inside the theatre the incident took place at a *dacha* on an estate outside Moscow. First reports suggest it occurred during a weekend shooting party, and involved an argument over a dead bird and the murder of one of the house guests.

Do we have any idea who committed this murder, and who the victim is?

The details are hazy. It appears to have stemmed from a bitter dispute over the casting of a new and controversial one-woman play. Apparently a celebrated actress from Moscow, a certain Irina Arkadina, had been overlooked in favour of Nina Zarechnaya, a lively young girl from a neighbouring estate who had dreams of going on the stage.

Do we know who was responsible for this decision?

Apparently there's a family dimension to it. The play's author, the radical young playwright Konstantin Treplev, is actually Arkadina's son. It seems Konstantin cast Nina in the role because he was in love with her, though it's said she didn't return his feelings.

And what do we know about the play itself?

According to Treplev he was exploring what he called a new form of theatre. It certainly sounds a pretty avant-garde work – something about a universal soul and the devil, I'm told. During the try-out in the estate's home-made theatre by the lake the audience quickly became restive. Matters came to a head when Arkadina denounced the play as 'decadent gibberish'. This apparently so angered Treplev he ordered the curtain to be brought down before the end. He accused his mother of being a member of a metropolitan elite, which claimed to have a monopoly on acting and writing talent. He then stormed off in a fury, at which Arkadina threatened to return to Moscow.

Is there any hope of a reconciliation between mother and son?

That's not yet clear. But there appears to be a further complication. Treplev had become extremely jealous of another house guest, Boris Trigorin, who was not only his mother's lover and a successful novelist but was worshipped by young Nina. She admitted to being a huge fan of his novels, while calling Treplev's play lifeless.

As a result Treplev burnt his script and fell into a deep depression about his ability as a writer.

A complicated story then. And how does the dead bird come into it?

Here suspicion has fallen on Treplev himself, who was seen earlier in the morning wandering around by the lake brandishing a gun. The bird, rumoured to be a crane, has been taken away for forensic examination, and a full report is expected soon. More details are promised shortly. Meanwhile back to you, Bridget.

Thank you, Michael. Michael Creasy there, our Moscow correspondent. If there are any further developments to the story, we'll come back to it later in the programme.

*

More details are now emerging about that sensational Russian murder story. Let's go straight back to Michael Creasy in Moscow. What can you tell us now, Michael?

Yes, Bridget, there have been some startling developments in this fast-moving story. It now appears that Treplev's acute depression prompted him to make a suicide attempt. It seems to have been something of a farce, as he merely injured himself slightly. There was then a rumour that he had challenged Trigorin to a duel, though we've not yet had independent confirmation of this.

It appears relations between him and his mother have been something of a roller-coaster. Apparently they were briefly reconciled, with Arkadina taking pity on her wounded son, but further rows between them followed, and a final rupture seems to have occurred.

Meanwhile a source close to Nina Zarechnaya has given us details of her plans. Apparently she had decided to follow her dream and try her luck as an actress in Moscow. She mentioned this to Trigorin, who, a well-known ladies' man, promised to meet her there. In this febrile atmosphere feelings on the estate seem to be running pretty high, with several cases of unrequited love and fractured relationships being widely reported.

Is there any news yet of the murder aspect?

Oddly, this part of the story remains shrouded in mystery, with no information forthcoming about either the victim or the assassin. People are remaining tight-lipped. But there are suggestions the theatre may issue a communiqué shortly, which it is hoped will shed light on this murky story.

Thank you for the moment, Michael. We'll hope to be able to report on the outcome of that communiqué in our evening bulletin.

*

Good evening. Let's go straight over to our Moscow correspondent Michael Creasy for an update on the Russian story. Michael.

Good evening, Bridget. Yes, the theatre has now issued that communiqué. But I have to say the mystery has by no means been solved. A body has in fact been found, and it turns out to be Treplev's. The official verdict states that he took his own life while of unsound mind. But there is widespread scepticism here among people I have spoken to. Why, they argue, should Treplev take his own life when he was at last getting published, and being seen as the coming man? They suggest this was not a suicide but a murder.

So has anyone been arrested?

Not as yet. The prime suspect is Trigorin, who had returned to the estate from Moscow after a disastrous liaison with Zarechnaya, and reportedly saw Treplev as a threat to his own literary standing. Suspicion has been fuelled by the fact that the remains of the manuscript of Treplev's latest work were found under his desk, torn to shreds.

Are there any other suspects in the frame?

I'm told the finger of suspicion has also been pointed at Masha Sorin, the daughter of the house. Trapped in an unhappy marriage to a local teacher, she had apparently long been in love with Treplev but knew that he remained passionately committed to Zarechnaya. She was addicted to snuff and known to have a drink problem, and there are suggestions that she could have committed the murder under the influence. It was also reported by one of the peasants on the estate that Zarechnaya, whose dream of fame had been shattered – she was currently involved with a third-rate touring company – had been seen wandering around the grounds that night. She allegedly had a mental-health issue, possible the early onset of dementia, so her involvement has not been discounted.

I assume the victim's mother is not considered a suspect?

Not only that but, strangely, it seems she is not yet aware of her son's death. The family are said to be shielding her from the tragedy, distracting her by plying her with drink and involving her in a game of cards – which they are apparently keeping close to their chests. Curiously, the dead bird had been returned to the family, and in stuffed form was found that night in a bookcase in the same room. According to the laboratory report, it had indeed been shot. However, it turned out not to be a crane but a seagull. Now back to you, Bridget.

Thank you, Michael. As soon as we get news of an arrest we will come back to the story. Meanwhile I understand you have some other theatre news.

Yes, there have been several announcements this week within the Russian theatre. Plans have been announced to turn Alan Ayckbourn's play *Sisterly Feelings* into a patriotic hymn to Soviet womanhood. At the Maly Theatre the adaptation of Dickens' novel *Hard Times* is entering its fortieth year, underlining the British writer's anti-capitalist credentials. There is to be an upbeat musical version of *Anna Karenina*, in which the heroine is prevented from committing suicide through her failure to buy a platform ticket at the station. And from St Petersburg we are getting news of the arrest of the controversial director Sergei Oblonsky, whose infamous play at the little Babushka Theatre, *When Vlad Met Leo*, about a homosexual affair between Lenin and Trotsky, has divided both the critics and the city's LGBT community.

Many thanks, Michael. And that's all we have time for tonight. Have a good evening.

A Holiday Humour

Edward was feeling cold and uncomfortable. It had been a long play. Lying on the floor of the box overlooking the stalls, he wondered how soon the theatre staff would finish clearing up and leave. He glanced at Felicity asleep on the floor next to him, her hair half covering her face. How strange, he thought, to be in this situation with someone I've only just met.

It was chance that had thrown them together. Edward and his sister Laura were in their second year at Bristol university, she studying Theatre and Performance Studies, he American History. Laura had booked seats for them to see an Ayckbourn play in Oxford. But then she had caught the flu so suggested Edward take Felicity, a fellow student on the theatre course.

Edward had hesitated. A shy, only child, his all-boys prep school and public school had left him ill at ease in the presence of girls. He was especially intimidated by his sister's extrovert theatrical friends. But Laura insisted. 'You'll find Felicity entertaining company,' she said. 'Anyway, you badly need a break from all this studying.'

Edward was a doggedly serious student, hard-working to the point of obsession. He had spent his first year buried in American History. He had attended all the lectures, read widely beyond the set texts, and worked into the early hours to deliver essays on time. He had become a fixture in the library, and rarely ventured out. He had no close friends, and certainly no girlfriend.

Felicity was his opposite. Essentially lazy, she did the minimum of work, plunging instead into the world of student theatre. Performing was her passion, both onstage and off, where she delighted in exploiting her considerable charm. Naturally gregarious, she loved to shock people with her outrageous opinions.

Having been briefed by Laura on Edward's character, she was determined to draw him out of his shyness and his preoccupation with his studies. Once the train had left Temple Meads station she talked animatedly about her hopes and fears, about her childhood, the tediousness of her lectures, the parts she had already played in student productions. She had won praise in a couple of supporting roles, and was planning to audition for Rosalind in *As You Like It*.

Edward listened attentively but said little, studying her features as she talked: her large, expressive green eyes, her tanned skin, and her attractive voice. He was shocked by her careless attitude to her studies but impressed by how easily she spoke of her feelings.

*

On arrival in Oxford she had suggested they take a walk before finding somewhere to eat. They strolled along the river path of the Isis in the hazy late afternoon heat and found a seat in the shade of a willow tree. A group of yellow ducklings was struggling to swim against the fast-flowing tide, the sunlight sparkling on the water. Felicity rattled on about the life she planned after university, and her determination to make it as an actress.

Edward was no more than politely interested. His mind was straying back to his studies. He was worried about his essay on Abraham Lincoln's complicated policy on slavery during the American civil war. Should he try and find a greater variety of sources? Did he need to make more of Lincoln's background? Would he finish the essay on time? Already he was regretting this trip, when he could have been extending his research.

Felicity brought him back to the present. 'I don't know about you, but I could murder a pizza,' she said. 'Come on.' Without waiting she stood up and began to move off. Edward struggled to keep up as she marched purposefully through the town.

*

They found a small, busy *trattoria* near the Playhouse, and a table by the window. Felicity insisted they order a bottle of wine with their meal. Edward rarely drank but felt ashamed to admit it. Felicity was frustrated at his continuing refusal to open up about himself. Once the food was ordered and their glasses filled, she decided to confront him. 'Tell me, Edward,' she said, 'don't you like women?'

Edward was taken aback. 'How do you mean?' he replied.

'Think about it. We've spent several hours together today. Yet I have absolutely no idea what you're thinking. It's impossible to engage with you at any level. Is it me, or is it my sex in general? Isn't it about time you came out of your shell?'

'I wasn't aware I was in a shell,' Edward said stiffly, knowing full well that he was.

'Oh, come on! Try unbending just a tiny bit. Look, you might even enjoy it.'

Through the window Edward watched the shadow of a cloud pass slowly across the Ashmolean Museum across the road. 'So what do you want to know?' he said finally.

'For goodness' sake, never mind what *I* want,' Felicity replied. 'Tell me anything you like – what excites you, what you're afraid of, the music you like, your feelings about your family, your ambition. The kind of things people normally talk about with their friends.'

Edward swallowed a mouthful of wine. 'I suppose I'm not brilliant at talking about myself. It's just that, well, most people seem so much better at it than I am.'

'Oh, to hell with other people! Let them listen to *you* for once. Just believe in yourself.'

'That obviously comes easily to you,' Edward said.

She laughed. 'I admit it. So why not use me as a role model?'

Edward felt the wine beginning to relax his mind. 'Perhaps I'll give it a go,' he said.

'Right. So here's to the new, outgoing, dynamic Edward!'

'Don't count on it,' he said, as they clinked glasses.

*

The Playhouse audience were quickly caught up in Ayckbourn's dark comedy, which skewered the tragicomic lives of its middle-class characters. Felicity led the frequent bursts of laughter that swept through the upper circle. Even Edward started to enjoy the many revelations that emerged. Certain moments reminded him of the hostile atmosphere between his parents that clouded his home life. During the interval he found himself tentatively sharing this memory with Laura, lifting the curtain a few inches on his childhood.

They had just returned to their seats when the stage manager appeared on stage. He explained that a key part of the set had become stuck, and it could take up to half an hour to sort out. The interval would be extended, and the management would meanwhile offer the audience free drinks at the bar.

Felicity was quick off the mark. When Edward finally battled his way through to the crowded bar she had already ordered two glasses of wine, and found two seats in a corner.

'You realise what this means,' she said. 'We're going to miss our last train back.'

Edward stared at her in dismay. 'Oh God, are you sure?'

'Absolutely. I've just checked on my phone. But don't worry, I have a plan.'

'You do?'

'We stay in the theatre while the audience leaves, hiding until everyone has gone and the theatre's dark. Then we find a dressing room, and a place to rest our heads.' She smiled. 'Maybe even a bed?'

Edward was thoroughly alarmed at this plan. 'But supposing someone finds us?'

'Oh, don't be so damn negative! It would be an adventure. The worst they could do would be to throw us out. Then it would be the station waiting room for the night. I've been there before now, and I can tell you, a dressing room would be a bloody good sight more comfortable.'

'I suppose so,' Edward said gloomily.

Once the play was finished they left the upper circle and searched for a hiding place. Dodging the ushers who were clearing the theatre, they finally found a door marked 'Stalls Box Right' and were relieved to find it empty. And so their wait began.

*

Finally the lights went out in the auditorium, leaving a single dim one piercing the darkness on stage. Edward waited for a few minutes, to make sure they were alone, then woke Felicity. They left the box, found their way through the stalls, and up the steps at the side onto the stage. They moved cautiously into the wings and through the backstage area, Felicity using the torch on her phone to light their way. But when they reached the dressing rooms they found them all locked.

'So what now?' Edward said. He felt suddenly exhausted.

Felicity thought for a moment. 'I've got it! Follow me,' she said. She led him back through the wings and onto the stage, now re-set for the first scene of the play.

'Do you see what I see?' she said.

Edward saw they were in the middle of a bedroom, with a sofa, two armchairs, and a double bed covered by a scarlet eiderdown.

'I do,' he said nervously, adding quickly, 'The sofa will do for me. You can have the bed.'

But Felicity seemed not to hear him. She had wandered to the front of the stage and stood staring out into the darkened auditorium. She felt the familiar rush of power that always came to her on stage. Imagining a packed house, eager to be enthralled by her magic words, she remained motionless for a while. Then she slowly turned round and walked upstage to Edward, who had settled on the sofa.

'Am not I your Rosalind?' she said, kneeling at his feet. 'Come, woo me, woo me: for now I am in a holiday humour, and like enough to consent.'

Edward shifted uneasily. 'Look, Felicity—'

She rose and sat down next to him. 'No, no, Orlando, men are April when they woo, December when they wed; maids are May maids, but the sky changes when they are wives. I will be more jealous of thee than a Barbary cock-pigeon over his hen—'

Edward stood up abruptly, crossed the stage, and stood a safe distance away. 'It's getting late—'

'Ay, go your ways, go your ways, I knew what you would prove. That flattering tongue of yours won me.'

'That's nonsense,' Edward said. 'What I mean to say is—'

'By my troth and in good earnest, and so God mend me, and by all pretty oaths that are not dangerous, if you break one jot of your promise, I will think you the most hollow lover, and the most unworthy of her you call Rosalind.' She rose and took him by the hand. 'But come, now I will be your Rosalind in a more coming-on disposition; and ask me what you will, I will grant it.'

'In that case just grant me a few hours' sleep,' Edward replied, pulling his hand away. Tired and irritated, he moved back to the sofa.

His prosaic words brought Felicity back to reality. She wandered over to the bed and sat on it.

'So how was my audition?' she said. 'Do you think I'll get the part?'

'What? Oh... I expect so,' Edward murmured.

'You don't sound very sure.' She climbed under the eiderdown and lay there for a while in silence. Then she called out, 'Edward? Are you comfortable over there? This is a very spacious bed.'

Edward kept silent, feigning sleep.

'Oh well. Good night, sweet prince,' she whispered.

It was some time before he really fell asleep.

*

In the early morning they were discovered. A kindly technician took pity on them after Felicity had wooed him with their story, and let them out of a side door without reporting their trespass. They caught an early train to Bristol and went their separate ways.

They never spoke again, aside from a brief greeting when occasionally they passed each other in the street or the university. But in the days that followed Edward began to look more critically at himself. He acknowledged the truth of Felicity's criticism of his emotional holding back. The following term he became friends with Maeve, a quiet, intelligent Irish student on his American History course. They hit it off, initially through their shared interest in the subject. But soon Edward began tentatively to talk about himself, even to dare voice his opinions, and their friendship deepened.

Carrying On

It's said you should never marry your leading lady. Alfred Stuart did just that during the second world war and lived to regret it. They were an ill-matched pair, he and Eunice Latham. They both had burgeoning careers in the theatre. But that just made things worse.

Their quick-fire romance began smoothly enough. On stage in the West End they were playing supporting parts in a popular long-running comedy, a young couple battling to overcome parental opposition to their marriage. Offstage their emotions were intensified by the everyday elements of war-time life: the air raids, the sirens, the hours spent in the shelters, the shattering loss of friends and neighbours.

But then Eunice became pregnant, and her worst qualities came to the surface. Self-centred, neurotic, and given to bullying, she was prone to intense jealousy and terrible rages. Alfred by contrast was gentle and kind, patient and cheerful, but essentially weak-willed; he did all he could to avoid getting involved in rows. Eunice's mother insisted he should do 'the honourable thing' and marry her, and he complied without argument.

They moved out of London to avoid the bombs and rented a farmhouse in Sarratt, a picture-postcard Hertfordshire village. During baby Michael's first year Eunice began increasingly to fret about her interrupted stage career. Once he was two, and starting to walk and speak, she became more desperate.

Alfred had been filming at Elstree Studios but was now rehearsing a keenly awaited new play in the West End, in which he had the lead. Because of the unpredictable train service, on weekday nights he stayed in London with an actress friend in St John's Wood. This infuriated Eunice, who resented being left alone with Michael for days on end, while Alfred forged ahead with his blossoming career. Her rages became frequent, and she started throwing things at Alfred – an ashtray, a coat hanger, a candlestick.

Alfred tried hard to pacify her but without success; her jealousy ran deep. He suggested they hire a nanny to ease her burden, but she didn't last long. A lean and sensitive Scotswoman, she was unwilling to put up with Eunice's bad temper; within a week she had given notice. Eunice turned to her sister Betty, who lived nearby. Betty loved children but had none of her own. Her husband Robin was away fighting in the Far East, so she was happy to stay with Eunice and look after Michael.

The minute Betty arrived Eunice pleaded exhaustion and took to her bed upstairs. But she soon got bored there and spent much of the day stretched out on the sofa in the sitting room, flipping listlessly through a pile of magazines, painting her nails, and listening to dance music on the gramophone. She ignored Michael, leaving Betty to feed him, take him out in the pram, prepare and give him his meals, and put him to bed.

When Alfred returned one Friday evening Eunice was in bed again, while Betty was getting the supper. He was just in time to read Michael a story. They cuddled up together on the sofa by the window, the low evening sun lighting up Michael's blond curls. Alfred read the story twice, encouraging Michael to turn the pages. 'And now it's your bedtime, young man,' he said. Michael resisted, pleading with Alfred to sing his favourite rhyming song. This he did, then took Michael upstairs and coaxed him to sleep.

Back in the sitting room he poured himself and Betty a glass of wine. She listened sympathetically as he talked of his week in London.

'There were several bombing raids, and yesterday there was a direct hit on some flats in Knightsbridge. It was terrible, there was flying glass everywhere, and one of our actresses received several nasty cuts on her legs. But today was quiet for once, thank God. Not a single siren. After the raid last night, people were trying to act normally amid all the rubble. But on the streets and in the buses and trains you could feel the tension.'

Eunice finally emerged for supper, still in her dressing gown, complaining of a lack of energy. Alfred was solicitous: 'No rehearsal tomorrow, my darling, so Betty and I can hold the fort while you get plenty of rest.' But the next day Eunice developed a temperature, and stayed in bed all day, eating little and sleeping fitfully. Her condition was the same on Sunday.

Alfred had an early start the next morning, so that evening, after listening to the nine o'clock news as usual, he joined her upstairs. Betty cleared the supper, then relaxed in front of the log fire. She dozed off but was woken by the sound of raised voices upstairs. She heard Eunice shouting but was unable to make out her words. Eventually the noise subsided. She waited, then ventured quietly upstairs to the spare bedroom.

*

Alfred woke early the next morning and crept into the bathroom. He scrutinised his face in the mirror: the blood had dried on the deep gashes on his cheeks. He wiped off what he could, but the cuts made by Eunice's nails were still visible. Dressing quietly, he ate a light breakfast and set out for London.

The walk across the village green and down the lane to the station was a part of the day he usually enjoyed. But today he scarcely noticed the trees and hedgerows, or heard the birds. How would he explain to the company the marks on his face? With the first night just three days away, how could they be hidden from the audience?

The train was for once on time. He avoided his usual carriage and, sitting among strangers, kept his eyes fixed on the *News Chronicle*, reading but hardly taking in the dispiriting war news as he thought anxiously about his injury. By the time the train arrived in London he had decided on his story. The gashes had been made by a stray savage dog that had attacked him in their garden, where Michael was sleeping in his pram. And yes, of course, a tetanus injection by the local doctor had already been taken care of.

At King's Cross he walked to the theatre rather than face inquisitive looks on the underground. He passed two bombed houses, their facades ripped off, leaving their rooms open to the elements. Police and hospital workers were sifting through the rubble, while stretcher-bearers stood by. Alfred gathered from a bystander a raid last night had killed several people.

Arriving at the theatre, he was relieved to find it unscathed. On stage adjustments were being made to the set, supervised by the stage manager. The actors were scattered around the darkened auditorium, waiting to start the rehearsal. Alfred made straight for the director James Shaw, sitting at his portable illuminated desk in the middle of the stalls.

James was shocked at Alfred's appearance. After he had heard his cover story about the dog, he reflected for a moment, looking closely at Alfred's face. Then he said, 'Sebastian has only had one understudy rehearsal. He's not ready yet. I'm sorry, Alfred, but you're going to have to carry on somehow. Let's talk to Jenny; perhaps her make-up wizardry will solve the problem.'

Backstage Jenny Cavendish, a large, warm-hearted woman, was helping with the actors' costume fittings. 'Oh Alfred!' she exclaimed. 'You *are* in the wars! Whatever have you been up to, love?'

Alfred repeated his fake story.

'Can you conceal the damage, Jenny dear?' James asked.

'I'll certainly have a go,' she replied. 'You poor man!'

She sat Alfred down in a chair in front of a dressing table with a mirror, and examined his face. She gently applied a layer of foundation cream, then different sticks of make-up, and a great quantity of powder. 'Does it hurt?' she asked.

'Not much,' he said.

But James was looking anxious. 'It won't work,' he said. 'The marks are still visible. Let's have another think and talk again at lunch time.'

During the lunch break Alfred had a beer and a sandwich in his dressing room. When James arrived he looked calmer. 'I've got it,' he said. 'We'll make a virtue of necessity. We'll cover the gashes with plaster and put a slip of paper in the programme, saying you've been injured by flying glass after a bombing raid but are determined to carry on. Would you be happy with that? I think it'll go down well with the audience.'

Alfred agreed. That evening at his friend's flat he phoned Eunice, but it was Betty who answered. She told him Eunice was better but was still in bed. Betty had been asleep when Alfred left home early that morning, so she knew nothing of his injuries. Alfred saw no need to worry her about them.

After a ragged dress-rehearsal – 'Always a good sign!' Jenny observed cheerfully – the opening night went off without a hitch. Alfred's first entry prompted a brief murmur from the audience. When he took his bow at the curtain call the applause increased, and there were shouts of, 'Bravo!' The critics liked the play, praising Alfred's performance in particular. They noted what one called 'his very English courage to carry on defiantly in the face of adversity'. The next day there were long queues at the box office.

*

That morning, with Eunice not yet stirring, Betty took Michael down to the village pond after breakfast, to feed the ducks and do her shopping. Later, as she was preparing lunch while he played with his toys, Eunice appeared. 'Did you get a paper?' she said abruptly.

'They only had the *Daily Mail*,' Betty replied. 'But there's a good review for Alfred in it. Apparently he had been slightly injured during a raid and was praised for carrying on.'

Eunice failed to respond to this news and grabbed the newspaper from the table. 'Daddy home now?' Michael asked her anxiously. Ignoring him, she hurried upstairs. In her bedroom, sitting at her dressing table, she read the review, then brooded in silence. She looked at herself in the mirror, applied powder to her face, and brushed her hair roughly.

She stood up, took a pair of scissors from her drawer, cut the page of the newspaper into pieces, and dropped them in the wastepaper basket. She took down from the mantlepiece two photos of Alfred, ripped them from their frames, and tore them to pieces. She paced up and down the room for several minutes, and finally collapsed on her bed, overwhelmed with self-pity.

Undercurrents

All right, Rosie, let's talk about your problem.

Thanks, Bill. I need your help badly. As you will have seen this afternoon, I'm struggling.

I was surprised. Last week in rehearsals you really made progress. I was believing in your Catherine. But now the tension and energy have suddenly drained away.

I know, I know.

Why is that happening?

Well, for a start, Trevor was desperately slow on his cues.

I noticed. Hungover again, no doubt. So what else was worrying you?

Selina's behaviour in the family scene didn't help. She seemed to have forgotten her moves, so I had no idea where the hell she was going next. That made me really tense.

That's understandable.

But to be honest, Bill, those were just minor problems. I was as much to blame as they were. I can't seem to… I really don't know… I think it's that Catherine seems such… such an elusive and complicated character. I can't get a handle on her. I feel all over the place. It makes playing Saint Joan seem like child's play.

All right, let's try to break it down. Here we have a very modern young woman facing a classic dilemma. She's torn between her academic career, her unfaithful lover, her loyalty to her family—

And her political beliefs.

…And her political beliefs. But she has qualities that enable her to deal with this conflict, doesn't she: determination, wit, and a shining intelligence. Fine: you're putting over those very effectively, as I knew you would. So after the first act we already sympathise with her. But that's just her rational side. What about her emotions, her fears, her vulnerability? I'm not getting much sense of those from you.

Oh God, I'm so aware of that.

Don't worry, Rosie. It's early days yet, and you're still on the book. I don't expect you to create a rounded character after just one week. But you do need to suggest her simmering undercurrents much earlier. That feeling that she's in danger of bursting out without warning – which of course she does, spectacularly, in the last act. You need to unearth that if you're going to get the dynamic of those final scenes right.

OK, but—

Look, darling, why do you think I cast you as Catherine? Because I know very well you have that danger within you – though you do a pretty good job of hiding it from other people.

That's because I hate losing control. I know exactly what's going on inside me emotionally; I just find it hard to project it on stage. There are places I want to go to, but—

Remember the actor's third eye? The idea that while you're playing a part, you're also watching yourself playing it?

Of course. What about it?

I think you're doing too much watching.

Yes. Actually you're not the first director to say that. The trouble is, I have no idea how to break the habit.

You need to dig deep into your basic fears, tap into your anxieties, explore your self-doubt. Use those darker feelings I know you have, which you try to keep hidden. Then you'll find you can access Catherine's inner life.

I hope you're right.

And you should work on that straight away. Tomorrow we're starting from where she breaks up with Kevin. Use that scene to explore these ideas.

I will try. Look, I'm really grateful, Bill. You've given me a lot to think about.

I'm glad of that. I'm sure you'll win through eventually. I have confidence in you, Rosie.

I know, I know. And that means a lot to me.

I'm glad.

Hold me then.

Breaking Through

SITTING IN THE small café by the river, Robert McFarlane watched the water flowing swiftly under Poulteney Bridge. He thought yet again how lucky he was to live in a city such as Bath.

He had moved here from London three years ago, seeking much-needed solace after his life had fallen apart. His wife had suddenly left him for a younger man, at the very moment when his daughter, whom he loved intensely, had started at university in Newcastle. The break-up affected his acting career, and his confidence in his ability. He realised he needed to start again, and leave London with all its associations and memories. With money from the sale of their house he had bought a flat in Bath, a city he had often visited and loved. Gradually his new surroundings – the elegant Georgian buildings, the spacious parks and gardens, the soft beauty of the surrounding hills – had soothed his damaged soul and helped him come to terms with his new life.

Now forty-five, he had eased imperceptibly into middle age. A solidly built Scot, his thinning red hair touched with grey, he had a friendly, outgoing demeanour, and was invariably respected as a good company member by his fellow actors, who liked and trusted him. Lacking any overwhelming ambition, his acting career had been only moderately successful. He had a good mind and was shrewd at analysing the essence of a part on the page but was not always able to bring it to life on stage. He had made his mark playing several middle-ranking Shakespearean roles – Macduff, Theseus, Cassio – and was content to remain at that level.

As summer shifted into autumn, a lack of work had brought back the acute loneliness he had experienced when he first arrived in Bath. But now he had landed the part of Leonato in a touring production of *Much Ado About Nothing*. It was not a play he knew, but in reading it for the audition he realised it was a substantial role. When he discovered the tour was to begin at the Theatre Royal in Bath, and rehearsals would be held in a church hall near his flat in Duke Street, his spirits rose further.

*

After the read-through on the first day of rehearsal, the director Mark Heritage talked at length about the play. He explained his decision to have period costumes and sets, and stressed the importance of clear verse-speaking. After suggesting a number of cuts, he spent the rest of the morning blocking the first act.

At the lunch break most of the company headed to

the nearest pub. Robert decided to use the time to go over his lines in his flat. He was having problems with Leonato's Lear-like tirade when he hears of his daughter Hero's alleged betrayal of Claudio on the night before their wedding. It was a ferocious speech that he knew would need him to exercise great control.

As rehearsals finished early he wandered over to the large bookshop in Monmouth Street, and bought a book about Elizabethan theatre. Afterwards, entering the café upstairs, he saw three of the actresses in the company sitting at a table by the window. One of them waved, and he went over to join them.

While they were considering what cakes to indulge in, Robert studied them carefully. Alison, the one who had waved, was clearly the leader of the pack. She was a large, exuberant middle-aged woman, with jet-black hair and heavy eyebrows that jumped up and down when she talked, which she did noisily, and often. Jemima, tall, slim, and elegantly dressed, was less raucous, but gossiped wittily with her about the merits and flaws of various men in the company, and made clear her disappointment with the director's very traditional approach to rehearsing.

The two of them had been cast as Hero's attendant women, Ursula and Margaret, and had already struck up a friendship. The other actress, Jane, was playing Leonato's daughter Hero. She and Robert shared scenes together, but they had spoken only briefly during the day's blocking sessions. Small, fair-haired, and neat, and clearly the youngest of the three, she seemed to Robert a quiet but friendly enough soul.

*

The rehearsal at the end of that first week focussed on scenes involving the merry war of words between Beatrice and Benedick. During a short break Robert noticed Jane sitting in a corner, a copy of the play in her lap. She looked forlorn and distracted. He wandered over and sat down beside her.

'Is everything all right?' he asked. 'You seem a little fed up.'

Jane emerged from her reverie and smiled wanly. 'Yes, I am rather.'

'Oh? Why is that, if I may ask?'

She paused, then said with sudden force, 'Do you realise how many lines Hero has in the first act?'

'I can't say I do.'

'It wouldn't take you long. Precisely one. All I do is listen to Beatrice and Benedick hurling witty insults at each other. There's nothing whatsoever for me to work on.'

Robert was startled by her fierceness. 'But things get better in the next act, don't they?'

She laughed bitterly. 'Oh yes? Act 2, Scene 1: one line. Scene 2: six lines, and then, after several pages of standing around like a lemon, a seventh. Just brilliant.'

'I hadn't realised you had so few,' Robert said.

Jane flicked through the pages of the play. 'Thank God for the speeches I have in Act 3! Though I reckon they're only there to move the plot along. The trouble is, there's no real scope for exploring Hero's character.'

'Are you sure of that?'

'Quite sure. First I witter on about my wedding dress. Then I'm accused of betraying Claudio but have little to say in my defence. Then I swoon, which puts me out of action for several scenes. Meanwhile everyone else gets on with the story. When I finally return from the dead, I announce to the world that I'm still a virgin. Great news. And that's it. Basically I'm just a feed for the other characters.'

Robert was surprised at her outburst. Something about Jane reminded him of his daughter Sarah. On an impulse he offered to discuss her part with her outside the rehearsal. She accepted the idea eagerly. They agreed to meet outside the Abbey the following morning and find somewhere to talk over coffee.

*

When they arrived in the Pump Room the musicians were playing a Beethoven quartet on the platform. Robert often came to this elegant, historic room to listen to the music. He thought it might appeal to Jane, and it seemed he was right. Sitting opposite him at their table, her head tilted to one side, she had quickly become absorbed in the music. When it ended she joined in enthusiastically with the applause.

'I'm really glad you brought me here,' she said, turning to Robert, her deep-blue eyes shining. 'It's such a gorgeous place, and I think the music is wonderful.'

While the musicians took a break Robert asked her how she got into acting. She talked easily about her family, and her ambition while still at school to work in the theatre, which her parents strongly opposed. She told him about her drama school, and how hard it had been to find work after she left. Eventually she had got a small part in a

TV adaptation of *Persuasion*, where she was noticed by an agent. Soon after this he had taken her on as a client and secured her the audition for Hero, her first stage role.

As she talked Robert was struck by her quick-fire intelligence, and her clear-sighted view of the insecurity of their profession. He was reminded again of his daughter, and a similarity in Jane's voice as she talked about her life. Then he remembered the reason they were meeting.

'I think it's time we had that chat about Hero,' he said.

Jane laughed. 'Oh yes, sorry. It had quite slipped my mind. I suppose we should.'

Robert noticed her reluctance. He sensed that the spell cast by the music was still affecting her. And now the musicians were returning to the stage.

'I tell you what,' he said. 'Let's forget about Shakespeare for now and just enjoy the music. If you're free tomorrow I could show you one of my favourite walks in the city, and we could talk more easily then.'

'That sounds fine,' Jane replied distractedly, her mind already back with the musicians, who were tuning up. As they began to play a lyrical Mozart quartet, Robert felt drawn to the music and pleased at Jane's delight in it.

*

On the Sunday morning they walked up to the canal that flowed along the hillside above the city. The water shimmered in the pale morning sun as they strolled along the towpath. A barge, decorated in bright red and green floral patterns, slid slowly past them, with a woman in a yellow headscarf at the helm. Jane, dressed in purple trousers and a sleeveless white blouse, waved to her, and the woman waved back. As a shaft of sunlight caught Jane's wavy blonde hair, Robert thought how very pretty she was.

Once the canal left the city behind it reached open country and meandered between green fields on either side. After a while Robert stopped next to a bench by the towpath.

'Time for Shakespeare?' he said.

'Good idea,' Jane replied.

They sat down, and Robert began the tutorial. 'Last night I took a close look at your scenes, and at two of them in particular. I think I can help you out there.'

'Oh, that would be *so* useful,' Jane said, turning to face him.

'Let's consider first your brief exchange with Don Pedro in the mask scene. It's the first hint Hero gives us of a merry element in her nature. This then becomes more obvious when you and Ursula plan to trick Beatrice. Hero is now speaking in verse, for the first time; in fact, the whole scene is in verse.'

Jane clasped her hand to her mouth. 'Oh my God, I was so busy learning the lines I hadn't noticed. Isn't that terrible?'

'Not at all. Anyway, now you're aware of it, look at her speeches again. They're not, as you thought, just a plot device. Hero starts to use similes and images; her thoughts are expressed poetically. She's no longer the demure, silent young woman but someone with a keen, observant eye and a mischievous spirit. Just notice how wittily and perceptively she spells out Beatrice's faults.'

'"So turns she every man the wrong side out".'

'Precisely. Suddenly she's become interesting, alive; Shakespeare has given her a personality. So here's your opportunity to flesh out her character.' He stopped, then added, 'Not to mention your chance to speak some very lively Shakespearean verse.'

Just then Jane noticed a family walking towards them along the towpath, the children kicking the gravel at their feet. She waited for them to pass before replying. 'This is all very exciting. I'm already seeing her in a much more positive light.' She sighed. 'It's so frustrating. I'm just not getting anything like this kind of help from our director.'

'Quite. Apparently Mark always leaves building their character to the actors. That's the way he works, and he's not likely to change now. I'm sure we're not the only ones in the company turning to mutual aid.'

Jane laughed. 'It doesn't feel very mutual to me. You're providing all the aid.'

'I'm more than happy to do that.'

'But it's so one-sided.'

Robert thought for a moment. 'There is one thing you could do for me, though.'

'Oh, do tell me.'

'You could hear some of my lines and read the other parts as we go through them. One speech in particular.'

'Of course. Willingly. But here?'

'It is a bit public, I suppose.' He looked around. 'We could go over to that field behind us. See that clump of trees in the corner? That should be private enough.'

They walked across the field and reached the trees. Jane took her copy of the play from her rucksack and sat down on the grass with it. Robert hung his linen jacket on the branch of a tree. Now that he was secure in his lines he wanted to bring out Leonato's fury with his daughter more forcefully. Being surrounded here by earth and sky, he thought, should enable me to let go, to express fully my rage.

Yet as he worked through the speech, he knew he was failing to convey the necessary emotion.

'Word perfect,' Jane said, when he finished.

'Words yes, emotions no. I need to try again.'

But the second time was no better. Some kind of barrier was getting in the way. 'Let's leave it for now,' he said, taking up his jacket. As Jane got up from the grass he said, 'There's an attractive pub a little further along the towpath. Do you fancy a drink there?'

'What a lovely idea. But only if you let me pay. To thank you for the tutoring. I insist.'

As they resumed their walk, Jane dropped behind to take a call on her phone. Robert reflected on his problem with Leonato's bitter speech. He knew he was struggling with the abrupt emotional shift, from showing his great love for Hero to his wishing for her death. But he now realised there was another factor. He was developing a fondness for Jane, and it dawned on him that this feeling was preventing him from expressing Leonato's anger with his daughter. The distinction between Jane and Hero had become blurred.

They reached the pub but found all the tables outside occupied. Jane went inside to buy the drinks, while Robert found a spot on the grass on the edge of the canal. He gazed into the calm waters, and then looked round at the fields and trees on the other side of the canal.

'This is bliss!' Jane exclaimed, arriving with the drinks, and sitting down next to him.

'It is,' Robert agreed. But he wasn't just thinking of the view.

*

Rehearsals were progressing slowly. Mark Heritage continued to focus on the actors' moves, their use of various props, and other technical matters. The actors muttered among themselves about his inability to discuss the sub-text of their speeches, but no one was prepared to confront him about it.

Robert struggled to keep his concentration during the long first scene, involving Leonato's exchanges with Beatrice and Don Pedro. Acutely aware of Jane's presence close to him, he was constantly distracted, especially when Leonato was required to hold Hero's hand or embrace her. Later he watched her scene with Ursula and was pleased to see how she was already capturing Hero's wit and verbal dexterity.

'You've cracked it,' he told her during a short break. 'As I knew you could.'

She grinned. 'I do feel I've got a proper part now. It makes so much sense suddenly. All thanks to you, of course.'

'But it's you who's done the work. You've really brought Hero alive.'

Afterwards he wondered how objective his view of Jane's acting was. As rehearsals continued and they talked often about the play together, he found himself admiring her sunny disposition, her curiosity about life, her wry sense of humour. Were his warm feelings for her clouding his judgement, he wondered?

Before long the rehearsals reached the scene of the marriage ceremony, and Leonato's shocking reaction to Claudio's accusation against Hero. Robert felt unusually nervous about the speech. As they waited to begin, Jane came over to him.

'I hope it goes well, Robert,' she said, with feeling, touching his arm. 'I'll be rooting for you.'

'Thanks a lot,' he said.

As he looked into her eyes, it struck him that she was not merely pretty but beautiful. But before he could say anything more the scene started. Having gone over his key speech again the night before, he felt confident he had found Leonato's anger. Yet as he delivered it he knew he was failing yet again. As Hero swooned and lay on the ground, it was still Jane that he saw there, not his daughter.

At the lunch break he bought a sandwich and a coffee and took refuge in his flat. What is to be done, he asked himself? How can I keep my emotions separate from those that Leonato expresses? The trouble is, I am thinking about Jane so much now. She's become lodged in my mind.

He heard the sound of a woman laughing in the street. Walking up and down the room, he pondered further. Then a thought struck him. Am I right to keep my emotions a secret? Why don't I just be honest and tell Jane what I feel? Perhaps that will help unlock my problem with that speech. But do I know exactly what this feeling is? I'm finding I miss her terribly when we're apart, and long to see her again. Can it actually be something as strong as love? And after the ridiculously short time I've known her? And at my advanced age?

The next day was Friday. Overflowing with these disconcerting and confused emotions, he suggested to Jane they might take another walk the following day. This time, he said, they could take in The Crescent, Victoria Park, and the Assembly Rooms. He was afraid she might have had enough of these outings. But to his relief she seemed as keen on the idea as before.

*

The next morning, as they walked together up Gay Street towards The Crescent, they came to a house with a poster outside, announcing 'The Jane Austen Centre'.

'Are you a fan of her work?' Robert asked Jane.

'Of course; who isn't? They're such brilliant novels.'

'It's odd that I've not noticed this place before. Shall we take a look?'

'Why not? It might be interesting.'

At the entrance a man and a woman dressed in period costume bowed and nodded to them in a suitably Regency manner. In the hallway they passed a life-size, romanticised waxwork of Jane Austen. 'Not much like her sister Cassandra's drawing of her,' Jane observed.

The first room, which housed an exhibition, was packed full of tourists, so they moved up a floor. The room here was a shop, with all kinds of themed merchandise on display. As they looked around Robert touched Jane's arm. 'Can I interest you in a Luxury Fretwork Jane Austen Tea Strainer?'

She took a look at it: 'I must confess I am more partial to that "I Love Mr Darcy Tote Bag", ethically produced in Thailand. What about you?'

Robert paused. 'I think it's a toss-up between "An Exclusive Emma Woodhouse Mug in Bone China" and a pack of "Jane Austen Tarot Cards".'

Jane smiled, and Robert felt a closeness to her, enjoying their shared mockery. As she moved ahead of him he noticed a 'Darcy Proposal Mug', inscribed with the words 'You must allow me to tell you how ardently I admire and love you'. It seemed like a sign.

Out on the landing they found a poster advertising the Regency Tea Rooms on the next floor up. They studied the menu, which included a Mrs Bennet Cake of the Day and a Lady Catherine de Burgh Proper Cream Tea.

'Do you know, I don't think I can cope with any more of this,' Jane said.

'Definitely time to go,' Robert agreed. 'I hate to think what she would have made of all this commercial exploitation of her name.'

Jane laughed gaily as they walked down the stairs. 'I'm sure she would have enjoyed satirising the whole ghastly business.'

*

They stood side by side on the wide expanse of grass in front of The Crescent. The building's mellow stone gleamed in the mid-morning sun. Jane gazed in wonderment at the stunning curve of the row of Georgian houses, then turned to Robert.

'What an amazing sight!' she exclaimed. 'It's quite breath-taking.' Robert enjoyed the fervour in her voice, and her delighted response to such beauty.

They moved on to nearby Victoria Park, with its gentle slopes and abundance of tall trees. It was one of Robert's favourite haunts. Often he would visit the aviary near the gate and watch the collection of small birds darting around their cages. He showed it to Jane but was taken aback when she cried out, 'Oh, the poor little things! I do so hate to see birds deprived of their freedom. Or any animals for that matter.'

'I'm so sorry, that was thoughtless of me,' Robert said. 'I didn't realise.'

'Oh, you weren't to know,' she replied. 'But I've always felt that way, ever since I was a child.'

'I think that does you credit,' Robert said, anxious to make amends.

Moving on across the wide-open spaces of the park, they reached a tree-lined path, the sunlight filtering through the branches. A group of boys were kicking a football around on the grass. Robert spotted a seat ahead of them and suggested they sit for a while.

He knew he had to speak now. Holding tightly on to the armrest of the bench, he took a deep breath – but just as he did so the boys' football came rolling towards them. Before he could move Jane was on her feet and kicking the ball smartly back to the boys. Returning to the seat, she noticed Robert's expression and laughed.

'You look surprised,' she said. 'I'll have you know I was the striker in our school team!'

Robert was thrown for a moment, unnerved at this

interruption. As Jane talked more about her schooldays, he gradually steadied himself. When she stopped he took another breath, and said, 'Jane, I have a confession to make. I think I've fallen in love with you.'

He saw the animated expression vanish from Jane's face. 'I'm sorry to spring this on you suddenly,' he continued hurriedly. 'I was so enjoying our friendship, but then, well, this powerful feeling gradually overwhelmed me. I just can't hide it any longer.'

Jane looked down at the path in silence. Robert felt his mouth go dry but plunged on. 'I know this must seem strange when I've known you such a little while. But I love being with you so much – in rehearsal, of course, but especially when it's just the two of us alone together, like today. The trouble is, these times go so quickly, and I feel so sad when we part.' He paused, then added, 'And you're so beautiful.'

Jane said nothing at first. Then she turned to face him. 'I'm not sure what to say, Robert. I'm very flattered, of course, by what you're saying. I do enjoy your company a lot, and I really appreciate your kindness in showing me round Bath. But beyond that… well, I'm not sure what you're expecting.'

'Nor am I really,' he replied. 'I just felt I had to be straight with you. You see, this feeling has caught me quite unawares. It's also affecting my acting.'

'How do you mean?'

'It's hard to explain exactly. I just get very mixed up, trying hard to hate you as Hero, when all the time I feel this love for you.'

'I hadn't realised…' She paused. 'You've been a great help to me with my part, and I do like you, Robert. But

I don't think it can be anything more than friendship between us. You see, I'm...'

She fell silent. Robert waited, but she offered nothing further. 'Right,' he said eventually.

'I'm sorry,' Jane added. 'But I'm just being honest with you.'

'I understand,' he said quietly. He felt suddenly awkward and embarrassed. He became aware again of the boys playing football, their voices forcing themselves into his consciousness.

Jane broke the silence. 'If you don't mind, I'd like to go back now.'

'Of course.'

They re-traced their steps through the park and past The Crescent, now in shadow. Lost for words, Robert felt a wave of sadness pass through him. He realised he had spoken out of turn, that he had put an unfair burden on Jane. And he had surely put paid to what had been a genuine friendship. So much for honesty! How reckless his confession already seemed. How stupid.

To his surprise Jane remained calm and eased the tension by talking calmly about the rehearsals. For this he was grateful to her – who was the mature one now? As they passed the Jane Austen Centre she even managed a wry smile. When they reached the Abbey she thanked him again for the outing, and they parted, the visit to the Assembly Rooms quite forgotten. Robert watched her walking away from him until she disappeared round a corner. Then he made his way slowly back to Duke Street.

*

That evening in his flat he felt confused and full of remorse. Let's face it, he told himself, she'll clearly never love me. But why should that be? Is it the twenty-year age gap between us? Perhaps there's already a man in her life? She's so naturally friendly and open, it would be surprising if there weren't. Maybe a relationship has ended recently, and she's wary of another one so soon? He agonised over these questions well into the night but found no ready answers.

When rehearsals resumed Jane seemed relaxed enough with him, and that made things easier. But he sensed a subtle shift in their friendship. Gone was her lively enthusiasm, her merry humour, and the abiding warmth that had drawn him to her. When they spoke together, she confined their conversation to the play. Robert struggled to match her apparent equanimity.

Soon the marriage scene came round again. Claudio duly accused Hero of infidelity, and she swooned. Robert experienced a rising feeling of anguish, which burst out on Leonato's opening line 'Hath no man's dagger here a point for me?'. He continued in this tortured vein, gazing down at his prostrate daughter and unleashing the full venom of a father shamed and dishonoured.

Reaching the line 'Why ever wast thou lovely in my eyes?' he stopped, overcome with genuine grief. Tears came to his eyes, and one of them dropped on to Jane's cheek as she lay on the ground. Startled, she opened her eyes, gave him a slight nod, and closed them again.

When the scene finished Robert felt exhausted but also exhilarated. He had broken through, she had understood, and she was glad for him. It was something.

First Thoughts

LET'S SEE, HOW does the story begin? An elderly actress (EA). Her sixtieth year to heaven. Her career on the skids; virtually no work. She's aged badly, physical deterioration – details? Or maybe she's retired, and life is lonely, empty. Perhaps her husband has died, or left her for a younger woman? She needs a comeback.

Her former agent is doubtful – her reputation for being 'difficult'. Is this justified? Give examples: never satisfied with dress or costume, unpunctual, tendency to upstage, etc. But agent is a loyal friend – he takes her back, finds her a small role in a classic revival (Priestley? Maugham? Nurse in Uncle Vanya?). What kind of production? Maybe staged in an old regional theatre – by the sea? Or a touring production? Must ponder pros and cons.

The opening – she's already well into rehearsal. Start story in bus taking her into town from her digs (describe?) to rehearsal room. She reveals anxieties about her part, her difficulty with lines. Reflects also on problems with young female director (YFD) – not just her gender but her use of improvisation, which EA hates – why? Bad experience in past? Not a creative mind.

YFD is unsympathetic, but wary of antagonising her – rehearsals are tense, awkward. Conflict between EA and the leading young actress (LYA). Describe. Who in the company is on her side? Perhaps a young assistant stage manager (YSM), his mother an admirer of EA. He hears her lines during lunch hours. She spills out anecdotes about past productions; he listens patiently; others are bored with them.

No, this scenario too complicated. Must narrow it down, find a better focus. Possible alternative plot: lack of work has left her anxious, depressed. Decides to devise a one-woman show. Options: a single character from theatre (Sybil Thorndike? Mrs Patrick Campbell?) or from literary life (Edith Sitwell? Ottoline Morrell?).

Or maybe a Shakespeare anthology, using parts she has played – and some she wishes she had played? Call it *The Ages of Woman* – a journey from Juliet to Nurse via usual suspects Miranda, Rosalind, Beatrice, Viola, Cleopatra, Emilia. Throw in a few stories from past productions? Just EA, a lectern, a glass of water, and the *Complete Plays* for support. No intrusive director, no competition for centre-stage with other actors.

Decide Shakespeare idea the most fruitful. But told from whose point of view? That of the actress, or omniscient narrator? Maybe a mixture, weaving in and out of her inner thoughts.

She selects programme alone, omitting only Lady Macbeth ('Ghastly woman'). Rehearses speeches in her flat, records them on a dictaphone, learns them by heart. But finds it hard to assess their effectiveness. Recruits a friend/retired voice coach (gay?) to provide comment, notes. He proves too critical; she dismisses him. Full of doubt, she selects different speeches, sticks to parts she has played before, and drops anecdotes.

A performance in her local arts centre. Only a small audience – a few friends, older theatre folk, drama students, a couple of casting directors, and her agent. Surprise: remembering her early success, she recaptures spirit of the younger roles. But struggles with older ones: they remind her of her age and her bleak existence. Her vocal mannerisms return, she loses the rhythm of the verse, and eventually dries. Ends up reading final speech from the text.

Dressing room – friends expected to come round but fail to appear. Removing her make-up in the mirror, she sees only the bags, the wrinkles. Decides impulsively to give up acting. Finally her agent appears – he's fixed another couple of dates.

Does she carry on? Or face reality? Leave open?

Desperately Seeking Miranda

I BECAME HER CAPTIVE the moment she spoke. At the traditional meet and greet she announced in a caressing voice: 'I'm Miranda Chambers, and I'm playing Titania and Hippolyta.' Her words hung exquisitely in the air as the other actors introduced themselves. I was so entranced I almost missed my turn. 'I'm Stephen Louden, and I'm playing Francis Flute the Bellows-Mender,' I murmured, feeling horribly self-conscious.

We were rehearsing *A Midsummer Night's Dream* in a gloomy church hall in Leeds. For the read-through the company were seated round a large table. I was opposite Miranda, which gave me a chance to observe her closely. She made a strong impression on me. Her round, open face gave her a humorous, almost mischievous air. She had curly auburn hair, swept back from a wide forehead, emphasising the attractive pallor of her skin. I noticed her small hands, slim and elegant like her figure.

Unlike the other actors, who were clearly saving their performance for later, she was totally immersed in her role, registering every emotion without restraint. Although she seemed to be reading the text, I guessed she already knew her lines. She brought terrific power and warmth to Titania's great ecological speech, 'These are the forgeries of jealousy', her voice vividly conjuring up the 'pelting river' that flooded the devastated land. When not involved in a scene, she concentrated firmly on whoever was speaking, her sparkling hazel eyes darting from one actor to the next.

The company spent the lunch break in The Angry Hamster, a spit-and-sawdust pub round the corner. Miranda sat with Cobweb, Peaseblossom, and others in her fairy entourage. I had a ploughman's and a pint with Snout the Tinker, who as usual droned on about his agent's shortcomings. I kept Miranda in view, absorbing her every gesture: the way she listened to others with her chin cupped in her hands, the graceful manner with which she tucked wisps of hair behind her ear, her tendency to grasp her neighbour's arm while making a point. Occasionally I heard her deliciously mellifluous voice rising above the chatter.

Back in the rehearsal room we went through the text again. Our director Jeremy Godwin suggested several small cuts. Some of the company resisted losing their lines, but Miranda calmly accepted her losses. She even suggested a couple of cuts herself, which I thought amazingly unselfish. Fortunately my part stayed intact, but then Flute has few lines – except, of course, when he plays Thisbe. And there's certainly no tampering with those immortal scenes.

As we broke up for the day Bottom the Weaver, a burly man with aptly flamboyant trousers, asked Miranda in his fruity, resonant voice, 'Fancy a drink, love?' She smiled and nodded. Outside it was raining, so she went in under his large, green umbrella. As I watched them walk closely together down the rain-soaked pavement, I wondered if they were an item.

*

We spent much of the next two days on games and exercises. For the mirror game we worked in pairs, copying each other's movements in turn. I was teamed with Helena, a tall, immensely serious actress with alarming dark eyes and a prominent chin. I found it hard to follow her actions while keeping an eye on Miranda, who was dressed in fetching green jeans and a dark-blue top, and had Oberon as her partner. I noticed how swift she was in her reactions to his movements.

Jeremy then asked us to create a backstory for our character. We had to tell it first to our partner, then the whole company. As one of the motley crew of 'rude mechanicals' of Athens, I was undecided about Francis Flute's backstory. What sort of life does he lead? What kind of home does he have? Is it in the suburbs of Athens or out in the forest? Is there much demand for bellows-mending in the area? Is he married? Does he have children? Perhaps he's gay or bi-sexual? This would explain his casting as the heroine in the Pyramus and Thisbe 'tragedy' that we mechanicals are rehearsing. 'What is Thisbe? A wandering knight?' he asks plaintively. He's clearly not studied his script properly.

In the end I decided Flute was a foundling, who had been discovered in a basket in the forest by a kindly middle-aged Athenian couple, who had adopted him. The husband was an experienced bellows-mender and had eventually taken the teenage Flute on as his apprentice. The man's hobby was wrestling, but after injuring his spine in a fall he had to give up work. Flute, to whom he handed on the business, had quickly gained a reputation for punctuality, speed, availability, good workmanship, and reasonable rates. He was soon in great demand within the bellows-owning community.

Recently he had been walking out with a plump Athenian girl called Pythia. To her great sorrow he had made it clear he felt unable to commit to a long-term relationship. I saw him as a late developer ('Let me not play a woman, I have a beard coming') and decided he had been roped into the production by his best friend Robin Starveling the Tailor. He had struggled to learn his lines, prompting our director Peter Quince's sharp rebuke: 'You speak all your parts at once, cues and all.' But he was a stickler for proper word usage, castigating Quince who, like Bottom, was much given to uttering malapropisms, such as confusing 'paragon' with 'paramour'.

Jeremy asked for volunteers to tell the company their backstory. Nervous as always of speaking as myself rather than as my character, I remained silent. But Miranda showed no such reluctance. Spelling out Titania's essential qualities with wonderful eloquence and wit, she spoke of her Amazonian feminist spirit; her passionate love for the countryside, imbued in her by her parents; her love of travel around the globe; and her continuing battles with the male chauvinist Oberon over her changeling boy. I took in her every word avidly.

The day ended with a quick ball-game, an exercise designed to test our reflexes and get us to bond more closely. At one point Miranda threw the ball across the circle to me. Contact at last, of a sort. But in my confusion I dropped it.

*

The next day we blocked the scene involving the first rehearsal of the Pyramus and Thisbe play. I had no lines here, which gave me a further opportunity to observe Miranda. Today she was wearing her hair up, offering me a glimpse of her small, charming ears, and her deliciously creamy neck rising above a beautiful, rust-coloured silk scarf.

Later in the scene Bottom entered wearing his ass head – stage management had managed to come up with a piece of temporary hairy headgear. We other mechanicals duly fled in horror, and then moved out front to watch Titania entice a transformed Bottom into her flowery bed – or on this occasion a battered green sofa. I studied their expressions, looking closely for any giveaway sign that they were intimate offstage. There was a certain amount of stroking of Bottom's hairy temples on Titania's part, and considerable horse play (ass play?) on his. But I could spot nothing that was not justified by the text. Yet I found their dialogue unnerving, especially when Titania confessed in rapturous tones to Bottom 'I do love thee'.

That evening, back in my studio flat, I re-played in my mind Miranda's vivid creation of Titania's backstory. I was rapidly falling under her bewitching spell and finding it hard to focus on Flute's scenes when she was in the room. Yet after a whole week of rehearsals we had not exchanged a single word. I might as well not have existed for her.

*

One day in the middle of our third week Miranda turned up uncharacteristically late. She looked paler than usual and seemed nervous. As Hippolyta, she and Theseus rehearsed the scene in their palace in the last act. Immediately she stumbled over lines she previously had word perfect and missed a couple of cues. She apologised, but when they worked on it again she was no better. After missing yet another cue she suddenly threw her script to the floor and shouted, 'I just can't cope with this *useless* Hippolyta woman! What the hell was Shakespeare thinking of, creating such a *thankless* part? She says virtually nothing, and just stands around while bloody Theseus hogs all the best poetry.' Turning to Jeremy, she added, 'You'll just have to find someone else to play her.' She strode off into a corner of the room and sat with her face in her hands.

Her words were so unexpected that even Jeremy, the most quick-witted of directors, was momentarily rooted to his chair. Finally, after suggesting we break for ten minutes, he went over to talk privately to Miranda. The other actors melted away or huddled round the coffee machine. I pretended to be texting on my phone, while trying from across the room to decode Miranda's body language. She was clearly very agitated and at one point in tears. Eventually she rose, picked up her shoulder bag, and hurriedly left the room.

The rest of the morning was spent rehearsing a scene between Puck and Oberon, but it had clearly lost its momentum. During the lunch break I took my sandwich to the local park, full of skateboarders and the occasional jogger. Sitting in the warm sunshine, I thought about Miranda's untypical outburst. Her fury about Hippolyta was clearly triggered by something outside the rehearsal room. Until today she had been so cheerful and resilient. I felt deeply sorry for her and speculated as to the cause. Was it due to some aspect of her personal life?

When we assembled after lunch she was still absent. Jeremy announced that Peaseblossom would take over as Hippolyta, and a new fairy would come on board shortly. This was a blow to me: I had looked forward to Miranda's Hippolyta being part of the audience when we mechanicals performed our melodrama at Theseus's palace. I had decided to play Thisbe for her alone, fixing my gaze on her at key moments in the action.

Jeremy then explained that Miranda's flat had been burgled while we were rehearsing yesterday. She had lost much of her jewellery and other items of sentimental value, and her cat had been seriously injured and had to be put down. Although she had resisted the idea, Jeremy had insisted she take the rest of the week off, telling her he could organise rehearsals round her scenes. Desperately upset, she had made it clear that she didn't want people's sympathy, as this would just upset her further. Jeremy asked us to respect her wishes.

*

She returned the following Monday. The other actors did their best to behave normally with her. In the days leading up to the technical rehearsal she eased her way back into Titania's skin. She regained some of her former confidence and was on top of her lines again. But her sublime humour had vanished, to be replaced by a visible sadness. Her Titania had lost much of her magic and become a more sombre fairy queen. Even her 'love' scene with Bottom had lost its merry element and become noticeably forced.

It so happened that my birthday fell on one of the rehearsal days, and as tradition demanded I brought in a cake. In cutting it I created a slightly larger one as a gift for Miranda, who was sitting chatting to Snug the Joiner. When I offered her the special slice, she looked up briefly, said, 'Not for me, thanks,' and resumed her conversation. We had scarcely made eye contact.

Deflated, I wandered back to the coffee machine and ate the slice myself. I felt desolate and rejected. I could find no way to establish any kind of relationship with her. My frustration cut me to the quick and started to affect my performance.

Previously, with Jeremy's encouragement, I had been playing Thisbe's ludicrous scenes with Pyramus in a melodramatic manner, indulging in a spate of 'bad acting' as might befit an Athenian tradesman. Now I started to play the scenes with real emotion, hoping this new-found poignancy would catch Miranda's attention. But Jeremy spotted what was going on and insisted I play the scenes the way we had agreed.

*

After four weeks' rehearsal we got into the theatre. As usual the technical dragged on for hours, with constant interruptions to adjust the lighting and sound. I watched Miranda's scenes from a seat near the front of the stalls. Miraculously, after all the difficulties in rehearsal, Titania's magic was suddenly restored. I was mesmerised all over again, and when it came to her final lines at the end of the play – 'Hand in hand with fairy grace / Will we sing and bless this place' – I was unable to hold back my tears.

The 'tech' had gone on until the early hours, so there had been no time to rehearse a curtain call. Just before the first preview Jeremy organised a quick call. Deciding to avoid the usual build-up from the bit parts to the leading actors, he asked us to just come on in a random way and take a couple of calls standing in a line, which we did.

When it came to the real thing that night, I saw my chance. I stood just behind Miranda in the wings and managed to steal in next to her in the line. I held her hand, which sent a shiver through my body. But after our final bow she turned to Puck on her other side and walked off with him, hand in hand.

For the following night Jeremy decided Oberon and Titania should be in the centre of the line for the call, and we lesser characters further out. But that one moment of physical contact had broken the spell Miranda held over me. Her hand had been delightfully soft and warm, and her proximity thoroughly enticing. But after that first thrill I had also taken in the smell of sweat emanating from her and noticed an ugly red blotch beneath her ear. In that moment she became a mere mortal. No longer the majestic and entrancing fairy queen, she was suddenly just an actress finishing a hard night's work.

While I continued during the rest of the run to admire her intelligent performance, my obsession with her had ended that night. Instead I found myself drawn to Lizzie McLeish, a small, dark, attractive Scottish actress, whose playing of Hermia I had scarcely noticed in my fascination with Miranda. I saw now how convincingly and skilfully she was playing that feisty, much-wronged young Athenian woman.

I had played Hermia's lover Lysander at school and wished fervently I could do so again. Then I could have got to know Lizzie and express my feelings for her under cover of Shakespeare's words. But I was stuck with Flute, so that notion remained a dream. All I could do, now that Jeremy was no longer checking up on us, was to put back the passion into my playing of Thisbe, and project it Hermia's way as I had tried to do with Miranda.

But when it came to the end of the run I had to face the disappointing truth: every night we played that scene Hermia paid more attention to Lysander than she did to my Thisbe.

Last Rights

THE TWO MEN emerged from the lift at the fourth floor. They walked down the long hospital corridor, the gloom broken only by the occasional reproduction of a well-known painting.

Paul Walwyn wore a suede coat with a fur collar. An experienced and ruthless theatrical producer, he was much feared within the profession. It had been his idea to visit Francis Cade as he lay dying. He was determined to secure the rights of what was clearly the writer's final play.

He had brought with him Daniel Ormond, a young actor who had scored in Cade's previous play. Lean, fair-haired and modest, Daniel admired Cade's work, and they had become friends. But now he was wishing he hadn't agreed to this visit. Walwyn had offered him money to support his attempt to gain the rights. This had upset Daniel's wife Ella. She thought the visit insensitive. That morning in her fury she had thrown a mug at him and hit him in the face. He could still feel the bruise.

They reached the relevant ward and waited to announce themselves. In a single side room Daniel Cade was sitting up in bed, his round face now pale and thin. Aged forty-six, he was facing his fatal illness with notable courage.

A young nurse appeared with a tray. 'Ah, Laura, I'm glad it's you again,' he said.

'My pleasure, Francis,' she replied. 'How are you feeling this morning?'

'About the same, thanks.'

On the tray were a pair of scissors, a small towel, and two oranges. She placed it on the bedside table and moved to the window. Opening it carefully, she turned back to Francis.

'By the way, you have a couple of visitors.'

'At this time? That's a surprise. Who are they?'

'A Mr Ormond and a Mr Walwyn.'

'Daniel again. I'd be glad to see him.'

Few of Francis's friends had visited him once his condition had worsened. Some were away and were unaware he was seriously ill; others were writing or painting, and didn't want to be upset. One man admitted he feared his eloquence so close to death.

'Shall I cut your hair first?' Laura enquired.

'You can do that while we talk.'

Laura nodded and left the room. Soon she returned with the visitors. While Paul Walwyn hung back, Daniel moved to the chair at the bedside and sat down.

'Good to see you again, Francis,' he said.

'You too, Daniel,' Francis replied. He adjusted his position in the bed. 'Thanks for coming. But where's Ella?'

'Oh, well.' Daniel hesitated, instinctively feeling his cheek. 'You know how emotional she gets.'

He turned to Walwyn and signalled him to come forward. 'Francis, this is the producer Paul Walwyn. He loves your plays – I thought you wouldn't mind if I brought him with me.'

'Not at all,' Francis replied, glancing at Walwyn.

Laura approached the bed. 'While you gentlemen talk with Francis I'm going to cut his hair.' She moved the bed away from the wall, tucked the towel into the neck of Francis's pyjamas, and set to work.

'Tell me, Daniel,' Francis said, smiling, 'what will you be doing in the spring? Building on your success, I hope. I'd like to know what your plans are.'

'It looks as if I'll be playing Young Marlow in a revival of *She Stoops*.'

'Excellent casting. You deserve it.'

'Do you know, Francis,' Laura broke in, 'your bald spot is getting bigger. We'll have to get you some ointment or arrange your hair very carefully.'

Paul Walwyn came nearer to the bed. He had heard that Francis liked directness. He also had a train to catch. 'Mr Cade,' he began, 'could I ask you what kind of value art holds for you now you are nearing the end of your life?'

Francis looked at him properly for a moment. 'Oh, I don't go in for grand statements,' he replied. 'I started writing plays by chance. I went on because I felt more alive doing that than anything else. That's all.'

Daniel started to earn his money. 'Francis, I know you don't like people talking about your public. But you must be proud of what you have done for other playwrights, and for actors like me. You've created a form quite new to the theatre, and that's very exciting.'

Francis brushed some loose hairs from the side of his neck. He leaned back and gripped Laura's wrist, a look of pain briefly crossing his face. After a moment he relaxed again.

'Goodness, Daniel, I do believe you've been listening to the appalling Rachel Stock. Why do you all admire that phoney journalist so much? It was that pretentious article of hers that made certain young playwrights believe they owed a debt to me. So at a stroke they lost all chance of developing their own voice.'

'I think you're being a little unjust, Francis,' Daniel said. 'What she wrote helped Logan and Warbey and Nina Eaton to get their plays put on in leading theatres. Isn't that worth something?'

'It's worth nothing to me. They have no true talent, but they think they have because she praised them to the skies.'

'They have perhaps been over-praised,' Walwyn said, 'but don't you derive—'

Laura broke in. 'Gentlemen, I'm afraid you'll have to step outside for a moment, while I freshen up Mr Cade, and give him a wash. He's sweating a bit—'

'Shut up, Laura,' Francis growled. 'I'm sweating because I'm angry. You can't send them out in the middle of our talk. You agreed to let me die in my own style.'

'I'm sorry to be a nuisance, nurse,' Walwyn said, 'but this conversation is of substantial significance – not just to those present but to the theatre generally.' He smiled at Francis. 'I was wondering if you derive a certain serenity from the fact that, though your contemporaries may not have fully understood you, enlightenment and praise will surely come from future generations.'

'Francis, be fair to yourself,' Daniel said. 'You must acknowledge you've made a great contribution to our understanding of the human condition?'

'Ha! Never! I've been allowed to get up late. I've ruined a few good instincts in myself. And I have three good friends to whom I can say anything. That's the only mark I've made.'

'Nevertheless,' Walwyn persisted, 'is not artistic achievement often quite divorced from a writer's intention or ideas? Many people thought your last play foreshadowed a new phase in your work.'

'Don't you mean a "broader canvas"? No, it's all rubbish. No more useless theatrical talk, please. It just embarrasses me and makes me angry.'

'With all due respect,' Walwyn continued, 'surely a writer has some responsibility—'

'No, he hasn't, whatever you're going to say. Another of those awful words and I shall start throwing grapes. Except nobody has brought me any today, thank God.'

Walwyn looked at his watch. 'I fear we must be going in a moment. I have to be in Bristol this afternoon. If you have any second thoughts…'

There was a silence, for second thoughts.

'Goodbye then,' Francis said. 'Goodbye, Daniel. Very good to see you. Thanks for coming.'

Daniel took his hand. 'I'll come again, Francis. Soon.'

'Sure.'

Laura shut the door behind them. Francis picked up one of his curls lying on the newspaper and studied it. Laura swept up those that had fallen on the floor.

'I didn't mean to shout, you know,' he said. 'Daniel's a lovely man and a talented actor. But all that talk from his friend.' He was silent for a moment. 'I wonder what he meant by second thoughts?'

'About your play, I suppose. He said he was a producer.'

'Ah, I see. Odd he didn't mention that.' He sighed. 'Oh, what the hell does it matter now? I shan't be here to see what people make of it. Or the wretched critics. Why don't I just let him have the rights?' He paused. 'Laura, ring down to reception and see if they have left yet.'

When Paul and Daniel emerged from the lift they were handed a message, asking them to return to the fourth floor. Walwyn smiled, strode back to the lift, and pressed the Up button.

Whipping-Girl

They were an odd bunch, the staff in our drama school. We were told most of them had been actors before. We reckoned they couldn't have been much good if they'd ended up working in a second-rate school like ours.

Among the teaching crew we disliked Barbara Drake the most. Every year in her class she had apparently selected a whipping-boy and consistently laid him low with her sharp, sardonic tongue. My God, could she let you have it! But in our year she made the mistake of choosing a whipping-girl. That was me.

Looking back, I can see why she chose to pick on me. Most of the students in our year struggled to cope with her withering remarks. Outside the classes they were openly critical, but during them they kept quiet, fearful of standing up to her and getting the boot. A couple of them gave up and left at the end of our first term. But I was different: in those days I was a brash, rackety student, full of confidence in my abilities. I was born with a competitive nature and a rebellious streak.

We heard from the second-year students about the background of 'The Drake', as they called her. She had played leading roles in a northern rep company, until a car crash had ended her career. It had left her with an obvious limp and a scar on the side of her neck. You would think this would have attracted sympathy, but her unpleasant manner made that impossible. A Scot well past middle age, with bright red hair and a deep, rasping voice, she was a forbidding figure, who used her walking stick as a weapon of menace to back up her constant criticisms of our work.

She made her teaching philosophy clear. Her basic aim was to make us forget ourselves. 'Leave yourself alone, immerse yourself wholly in the character,' she said. This seemed to me to be just plain wrong: how could you *not* make use of your personality? I was bold enough to question her idea. I said you obviously have to draw on your own qualities as well as those of the character you're playing. That's when she singled me out for special treatment.

From then on she picked me up on everything – my movement, my voice, my breathing technique, my posture. She especially took me to task for my opinion about Stanislavsky's ideas, and all that stuff of his about Objectives, Obstacles and Actions. I thought it was simply common sense, and I told her so. She was furious. She said I had wilfully failed to understand his whole system's fundamental value and purpose. She also liked to have a go at my clothes. 'Why are you dressed like a prostitute?'

she asked me once, when we were rehearsing a Shaw play. How nasty was that?

My friend and fellow student Alice and I shared a poky little flat in a rundown area of the city. Our lack of a grant meant we lived on a diet of instant coffee, fish and chips, and tinned fruit. A small, very sweet but shy girl, Alice was amazed I could stand The Drake's constant battering. But I was used to standing up for myself.

Things came to a head over the Emotional Truth exercise. For this you had to recall a traumatic experience in your life, then face the other students' questions about it. 'The intention,' The Drake explained, 'is to shed your own personality, to go all out for emotional truth in recalling your experience.'

I offered to tell a story about my dad locking me in the cellar for a whole day when he discovered I had bunked off school. The Drake accepted my choice with a curt nod. But actually there was no trauma; my story was a pure invention. My sweet old dad, who loved me dearly, would never have treated me like that.

I calmly explained that in the cellar I had found a pile of newspapers and magazines waiting to be recycled, and had really enjoyed the hours spent reading them. I had survived by plundering some of the food and drink that had been laid in for Christmas: a box of mince pies, a chunk of stilton, a bag of pistachio nuts, and several cans of beer.

After I told my story the questions began. Naturally I found it easy not to become emotional about something that never happened. I described the day as a welcome change from school, a merry lark. That was when The

Drake stopped me. Her face was a right old picture. 'That was completely inappropriate and a total waste of time,' she shouted furiously, waving her stick in anger and storming out of the room.

Her revenge came at the end of the year. We were to stage scenes from *Hedda Gabler* to an audience of friends, actors and agents. I reckoned Shirley Ellis, the most talented student in our year, would be a dead cert for Hedda. But I was confident of being chosen for Mrs Elvsted, the second largest female role. So imagine my feelings when the cast list went up on the notice-board, and I found I was only down to play Hedda's servant Berte. Ibsen described her as 'getting on in years, with a homely, rather countrified look'. She had just two scenes, and even these I had to share with Lily O'Hara, who was playing Hedda's aunt, Miss Tesman.

I knew the casting had been done jointly by three of our teachers, including The Drake, who was to direct the production. I was sure she was behind the decision to give me such a miserable role. I quickly devised a plan for revenge. Alice was desperately worried when I told her about it. 'You'll probably be kicked out if you go ahead,' she said. I told her I was getting so little out of the course I couldn't care less.

During rehearsals I was a model of good behaviour. I played Berte exactly as the text suggested. A gentle, subservient country woman, who had previously worked for the elderly Miss Tesman, she was apprehensive about her new employer, Hedda Gabler.

By now I had realised that directing was not The Drake's forte. She was one of those authoritarian directors with very fixed ideas, and her brusque manner left the students no space to suggest their own. For my scene which began the play, she decided Miss Tesman should be a dim, restless, and slightly neurotic character, over-impressed by her brother Tesman's scholarly status. Lily tried to put this characterisation into practice. The result, I thought, was a mannered and superficial piece of acting. But it played into my hands.

When it came to the performance I was determined to make Berte the centre of attention. On my entry I dropped the bouquet of flowers I was holding and made a meal of picking them up. I gave Berte a more forceful character than before, adopting an insolent tone when speaking to Miss Tesman. I could see Lily was taken aback by this change, but she managed to keep going. I followed her round the room, imitating her walk and her gestures at moments when she wouldn't notice. There was sporadic laughter from the audience, which puzzled Lily. To underline the new Berte, over my dull grey servant's costume I wore a vivid red sash round my waist.

'What the hell were you playing at?' Lily asked me afterwards in the wings. I told her I was bored with The Drake's production and wanted to liven it up. She was understandably annoyed, but I was exhilarated by my performance. I looked forward to The Drake's reaction, but there was no sign of her backstage.

The next morning I found two letters in my pigeon-hole. One was from the principal. He wrote that after a lengthy talk with Miss Drake about what he called my irresponsible behaviour, he was ending my involvement with the school. There was all the predictable stuff about letting down the school and my fellow students. He made it clear I could not expect a reference.

The other letter was from an agent, Lesley Swift. She had apparently been impressed by the original way I had played the opening scene of *Hedda Gabler* and asked me to come and see her in her Holborn office. She told me I had great promise, and we hit it off immediately. I became a client. She got me my first job and then my Equity card. And it's to her that I owe my successful career over the last ten years.

Last month I bought a ticket for my latest West End show and sent it to The Drake, whom I heard was still teaching at the school. I don't know if she came, but I hope she did. This time I was not playing Berte, nor even Mrs Elvsted, but Hedda Gabler herself.

The Case of the Missing Doll

The train crawled in to Hartley Gossamer station around noon. I hit the empty platform and looked around. No sign of a cab, so I took my feet down the lane to the village. Clouds were drifting high in the summer sky. A bird uttered the kind of song that birds go in for. Someone was making with the church bells.

I reached the main drag and checked the green-edged business card: 'Mandy Carver, Hartley Gossamer Arts and Crafts'. I found the joint in question and moved inside. The place was heavy on antiques but light on customers. Behind a counter a cream-faced blonde was deep in a magazine. The air was thick with silence and the smell of face powder. I was expecting some manners, but she didn't have any. If there was any energy about, I had brought it with me.

A handwritten notice at the back read 'Arts and Crafts Upstairs'. I climbed the wooden spiral staircase. Another counter, another woman. Except this one was a brunette and as wide awake as you can be in a sleepy English village. I put her in the late, late thirties. She was wearing a caftan, a string of jade pearls, and a deadpan expression.

'Miss Carver?' I enquired. She nodded. 'Webster. Jack Webster. You called me.' She made good use of her harvest-brown eyes. They were the kind that made you like being stared at. I gave her my private investigator card, the one without the photo of a gun on it.

'Ah, Mr Webster. Let me get you a coffee,' she said.

'Make it an Americano,' I replied. I needed to keep my lids open.

The room was stuffed with bright woollen scarves and hats, tables of fake-looking jewellery, rows of handmade pottery, paintings of scenes from rural life. I parked my body in a hard Windsor chair and waited. The minutes crawled by like a wounded rabbit. I lit a cigarette, then killed it, and strolled to the window. The streets were deserted. It was so quiet you could hear a horse sigh in the next village.

Carver and her eyes came over with two cups of coffee. She gave me one and eased her body down on to a chair opposite me. I looked into a face that had seen worse days. 'So what gives with the mystery?' I asked. She offered me a down payment on a smile.

'Sorry I couldn't say more on the phone, Mr Webster. I need your help.' Some days it pays to leave the white charger in the stable. I had a hunch this might be one of them. She caught my hesitation and drew a sheaf of readies from her handbag.

The Case of the Missing Doll

'I'll double your normal fee,' she said.

I nuzzled my coffee and leant forward. 'The dough is not important, lady,' I snarled. 'Just put me in the picture.' Dames think they can get you with the folding. But a shamus needs to sleep easy at nights.

She took a lot of moments to weigh me up. Her eyes said I passed the test. 'Are you familiar with Shakespeare, Mr Webster?' she asked.

I leant back in my chair. 'Culture's not my business, lady. I'm a private dick. I find things out. That's what I get paid for. Just give me the dope.'

'Of course,' she said, fixing me with those eyes again. She had two expressions – cool, and very cool. 'Let me explain. I'm the director of the local amateur dramatic society, the Hartley Players. We put on plays in the village hall. At the moment we're rehearsing part two of *Henry the Fourth*.' I'd missed out on part one, but I let that pass. 'Jinx Lincoln, who's playing Doll Tearsheet, has gone missing. I want you to find her.'

That was the nutshell version. I needed more if I was to dig the dirt. She gave it to me in spades. I listened hard. Seemed like this Doll character was some kind of broad in this Henry play.

'There's been no sign of her for three days,' Carver said. 'No sight of her in the village bookshop where she works, no answer on her phone, no sign of her car, a blue Volkswagen Beetle. She has a boyfriend in the village, Jason Lightbody, but he's on holiday.'

She gave a version of a sigh and took a slug of her coffee. 'She's normally very reliable. I can't think why she's disappeared. As far as I know she wasn't in any trouble. I can't imagine anyone would want to harm her. She's a talented, lively actress, popular with the company, and very musical. She was an obvious choice for Doll Tearsheet. Nicki Harper is standing in for her, but she's not a patch on Jinx.'

I asked the obvious question. Like why hadn't she called in the local prowl boys? She gave a shrug. 'That's simple; there aren't any. The nearest police station is five miles away. Just three men and one woman to cover Hartley Gossamer and six other villages. Unless it's a question of murder, you have to join the queue. I don't have time for that, which is why I got in touch with you.'

We closed the deal, and I began to earn my fee. I told her I needed a photo of the missing dame. She slid across the room to a row of mug shots on the wall. I joined her in front of the rogues' gallery. 'This is her in our last show,' she said. She pointed to a smart-looking cookie with neat regular features, pencil-thin eyebrows, and a cupid's-bow mouth. She had a bundle of charm in a low-down sort of way. It was a start.

*

Carver had booked me a room for the night in the village pub, The Brass Monkeys. She gave me the address of the bookshop where this Lincoln dame worked. It seems the guy to button-hole was the manager, Terry Sanderson. I strolled back down the main drag, past rows of quaint little cottages and shops. It was real picture-postcard stuff. A far cry from the mean streets of downtown LA.

I found the bookshop down a cobbled alley. 'Books For Ever' read the hopeful sign above the window. A bell jangled over my head as I entered. Behind the desk a man was arguing with a woman about the price of a book. He wore a scarlet cravat and had a voice like a muffled chainsaw. Before putting the bite on this bird I took a sniff round the joint.

It was a labyrinth of dusty rooms. Books were stacked in untidy heaps on the tables and floor and shelves. At the back I found the 'Crime Fiction' section. My kind of territory. It was full of the usual suspects: Agatha Christie, Ngaio Marsh, Dash Hammett, Ray Chandler, Dorothy Sayers, Erle Stanley Gardner – the whole goddamn pack of them. I settled on a Chandler paperback and took it over to the guy at the desk.

'Mr Sanderson?'

He had thick black hair and heavy jowls; his tweed jacket had seen better days. I filled him in on my assignment. 'Jinx Lincoln?' he said, his eyes narrowing. 'Not exactly an ideal assistant. Much too inclined to dream. And punctuality was certainly not her strong suit. I had to have words with her. And now she's left me in the lurch, damn her.'

'Any idea where she might have gone?'

'None at all, unless she's crawled back to the family home.'

'And where is that?'

'Somewhere outside Gloucester.' A scornful smile twitched at the corner of his mouth. 'She comes from a wealthy family.'

Nuts to him, I thought. I paid for my book and left.

*

Carver had suggested I talk to her actors. They were rehearsing that evening in the village hall. That gave me a couple of hours to kill. I spent them in the saloon bar of The Brass Monkeys, in a corner beneath the oak-beamed ceiling.

High on the brick walls hung rows of pewter mugs and coloured plates. Below them were sepia shots of Victorian folk, standing in the street and staring suspiciously at the camera. An old poster above the bar listed the Rules of the Inn: 'No Thieves, Fakirs, Rogues or Tinkers', 'No Slap and Tickle of the Wenches', and 'Flintlocks, Cudgels, Daggers and Swords to be Handed to the Innkeeper for Safe-Keeping'. To hell with those goddamn English rules. I kept my gun in my pocket.

Pulling on a bourbon on the rocks, I started to read my thriller. As usual with Chandler, it was a sweat to follow the plot. I ditched it and picked up a copy of the *Hartley Gazette*. 'Vicar condemns altar wine theft' was the front-page lead. Inside was a heap of local stuff: farming news, church services, court cases, and a shed-load of petty larceny. The back page ran items for sale: Victorian fish knives, second-hand croquet balls, clogs direct from Sweden. That kind of junk.

I emptied my third bourbon and checked the ancient clock on the wall. It was time to breeze. I wandered across the green, past the rusty village pump, and up the hill to the hall. It was an ugly-looking red-brick joint, set back from the street. Carver was waiting for me in the hallway.

She showed me into a small side room. It was crammed full of props, costumes, a couple of chairs, a worn carpet, and a battered purple sofa. 'I've spoken to the actors,' she said, handing me a sheet of paper. 'Here's a proof of the programme containing the cast list. I'll send them in when they're free. Go carefully with them, Mr Webster. They're a sensitive bunch.'

First in was good King Henry himself. Hell, even in a missing-persons case royalty gets priority. I wondered whether to bow but decided against. He said his name was Jimmy Spittle, and I had to believe him. Tall and bulky, with olive skin and a trim goatee beard, he had a handshake that rearranged your fingers. I could see why he was cast as top banana. He spread his ample body on the sofa: it wasn't a throne, but at least it was purple.

'I liked Jinx a lot, but I found her unpredictable,' he began, in a deep bass voice. 'She tended to blow hot and cold. She was warm and friendly one moment, and the next she was distant. I felt her mind was elsewhere. It's affected her acting in recent days.'

'In what way?'

'She was a merry Doll Tearsheet, relishing the character's fruity language. But at the last rehearsal she seemed to be speaking mechanically. Her heart clearly wasn't in it.'

Exit the king, enter the number two Doll. This Harper dame had red hair, green eyes you wouldn't fool with, and a good line in shoulders. Her clothes did her no harm; they fitted her well. Turning a chair round she sat astride it and threw me a cool, smouldering look. She was a cute little trick, with a pair of legs that were not painful to look at. Women don't have many lines of attack, but those they have they keep well-polished. I left plenty of space between her and my professional standing.

'So tell me, sister, how well did you know Jinx Lincoln?'

'Hardly at all until this production,' she purred. 'I'm new to the Players. But as her understudy I had a good chat with her about Doll's character. After that I watched her carefully in rehearsal.'

'How would you rate her as an actress?'

She hesitated. 'She has a good voice.' Another pause. 'She's quick to learn her lines.' It wasn't a heap of praise.

'And offstage? What kind of person is she?'

'Oh, she's much liked,' she said, with a thin smile. 'Especially by the fellas.'

'I gather she has a boyfriend? Do you know him?'

'Jason?' She shrugged. 'I've seen them around together.'

'Any idea where she might be?'

She shifted uncomfortably in her chair. 'Not a clue.'

She was playing hard to get. She rose, smoothed her skirt down, and slinked to the door. 'Sorry I can't help any further,' she said. 'I'm needed on stage.' A final glance over her shoulder, and she was gone.

Next in was a guy with a lot of face and chin. He introduced himself as Pistol. What kind of handle was that? I instinctively slipped my hand into my pocket, then relaxed.

'Jasper Lennox in real life,' he said, clocking my surprise. 'I always get the comic character parts, but that suits me just fine. You see, I have a flair for comedy. Even at primary school I had a reputation as a mimic. I think I inherited it from—'

I stopped the guy in mid-flow. 'That's fine and dandy, Mr Lennox, but this is an investigation, not an audition. I need you to play ball. Let's talk about Jinx Lincoln.'

'Very well,' he said stiffly, licking his puffy lips. For a self-styled comedian he seemed to be short on a sense of humour.

'Did you know her well?'

'I wouldn't say that,' he muttered sourly.

'So what would you say?'

'Well... I found her prickly. Not too good at taking criticism.'

'For instance?'

'Only last week I tried to give her some help. She was struggling with her lines, so I decided to give her a hand. I told her about my well-tried memory device, which I've refined over the years. First of all—'

I reined him in again. 'Cut out the wise talk, mister. Just get to the prickly bit. And make it snappy.'

His face shifted into sulky. He was starting to shred round the edges. 'I couldn't believe it,' he sneered. 'I like to give youngsters the benefit of my experience. But she said she wasn't interested in that kind of trickery – that was the actual word she used. Trickery! I was mightily offended, I can tell you. After all—'

'One final question, bud. Have you any idea why she's missing?'

He took a moment to control his irritation. 'None whatsoever,' he said finally. 'And as far as I'm concerned, she can stay missing. Her understudy Nicki is much more approachable, and quite happy to take a hint or two from an old pro like me.'

It seemed a funny label for an old amateur to use. He was in a huff, and he left in it. I saw other members of the cast, but no dice there. Seemed I was going to end up with the big round O.

Last on my list was Brenda Cummings, marked down as playing a dame called Mistress Quickly. A large, well-fed woman, I reckoned she had left fifty behind some time ago. She had a warm, generous face, and big blue eyes. She went all human on me, and the words came pouring out. This time I let them flow.

'I do hope I can help you, Mr Webster. It's so upsetting about Jinx. She's a real sweetie, and a good actress too. I have several scenes with her, and she's fun to play off. Never quite the same from one rehearsal to the next, but I like that, it keeps me on my toes. Offstage too we bonded rather well. We share the same star sign, and that helps. We're Leo, you see.'

I didn't, but to hell with that. 'Did she seem at all anxious recently?'

'Not at all. She was full of beans, as usual.'

'And when did you last see her?'

'The day before she disappeared. She was driving through the village, and she waved to me. She seemed very cheerful.'

I liked this Cummings dame: she played it straight down the line. I gave her my card, told her to get in touch if anything came up. After that I hung around in the hallway until the rehearsal ended. As the actors vanished into the night I put Carver in the picture.

'We badly need a breakthrough,' she said, when I had finished. 'I suggest you pay a visit to Jason's mother, Molly Lightbody. She has a council house on the edge of the village. I've told her what you're doing. I'll give you her address.'

I walked back down to The Brass Monkeys. A crescent moon was hanging up in the darkening sky. In the pub a handful of villagers were still at the hooch and the gossip. I left them to it. The head honcho showed me to my room. It didn't go a bunch on home comforts, but it was somewhere to shut the eyes. It had been a lot of day, and I needed to connect my head to the pillow.

*

In the morning I put on clean linen and ordered the full English breakfast. I asked for my eggs to be hard boiled. They arrived along with a plateful of everything. I washed it all down with a cup of strong black coffee. It helped to prise my eyes open.

Out on the green the sun was doing its best to shine, which wasn't much. Mrs Lightbody's house was in a street well away from the village centre. The doorbell played a tune I didn't recognise. Through the frosted glass I made out the outline of a body pausing by the door. She took a whole lot of time to open it, and then only by a crack. 'Yes?'

'Good morning. I'm Jack Webster. I've come about Jinx Lincoln. Mrs Carver said you'd see me.'

'Ah yes,' she said. She gave me the once-over, took the chain off the latch, and showed me into her sitting room. 'You'll have to excuse the mess, but I'm having a bit of a spring clean.' I believed her, even though it was summer.

Tall and thin, she was wearing a blue plastic housecoat, pink slippers, and a pair of rimless glasses. They gave her the look of a disappointed librarian. She gestured towards an armchair and offered me a sherry. I declined: a shamus has to draw the line somewhere. She poured herself one from a cut-glass decanter, then sank wearily into a leopardskin-upholstered sofa.

'How can I help?' she asked, stifling a yawn.

I moved straight in. 'I gather your son Jason goes around with Jinx Lincoln.'

'That's right.'

'How long have they been together?'

She took a long time to answer. Her eyes seemed to be closing. 'I suppose about a year or so,' she said finally. 'After he finished with Nicki Harper. Actually I'm surprised it's lasted so long. Jason's a bit of a butterfly when it comes to girls, if you know what I mean.'

I did. 'Have they had any disagreements recently?'

'Not that I'm aware of. I think I would have known if they had.'

I pressed her further, but she was already losing interest. She started to tell me about her husband's allotment. Her eyes began to droop, then closed. I took my cue and let myself out.

*

I dug around some more. I put the screws on the vicar, the pub landlord, the dame running the mobile library. No one came up with the goods. The Lincoln dame was as missing as she had ever been. My investigation was going nowhere fast. It was time to wave goodbye to Hartley Gossamer and all who sailed in her. I picked up my fee from Carver, apologised for the failed assignment, and

The Case of the Missing Doll

headed for the station. I needed to get home and count the spoons.

I arrived as my train was pulling in. It was due to leave in ten minutes. A handful of passengers got out. Most of them were elderly, except a brightly dressed young couple, each holding a suitcase. The girl's face matched that of Jinx Lincoln. I confronted her at the station exit.

'Doll Tearsheet?' I said. 'Jack Webster, private investigator.'

She reddened and sat down abruptly on the bench nearby. The young man joined her there. I spilled them the dope about my mission. 'Oh God, I knew I was letting the production down,' she sighed, 'but our plan seemed much more important.' She spoke so quietly I only just caught her words.

'And what exactly was this plan?'

She looked at the young man. 'You explain, Jason,' she said, and began to cry.

I gathered this dude was the notorious butterfly. He had shoulder-length hair, a heavily freckled face, and was filling a black leather jacket and faded denims. He put his arm around Lincoln and looked coolly at me.

'If you must know, we've just got married. We wanted to keep it a secret, to avoid all the village gossip.' He hesitated, then added, 'Jinx is pregnant, you see. That's going to make life bloody hard for us here. So we wanted to delay telling people as long as possible.'

I could see their point. Small towns with small minds are the same wherever you park your body. I went over to the red phone booth nearby and called Carver.

'Webster here,' I said. 'I'm at the station. I have your

Doll Tearsheet with me. She's coming to see you now. She'll explain everything.'

I listened to Carver's words of relief and thanks, then returned to the couple. The Lincoln dame was drying her eyes. I told her she should spill the beans to Carver first thing. She agreed. I watched the pair of them walk away down the lane towards their future.

I returned to the platform as the guard was blowing his whistle. I jumped aboard and found an empty carriage. The countryside began to gather speed through the dusty, sun-flecked window. I sat back and chewed over The Case of the Missing Doll.

It was one of my easier ones. I still belonged to the human race, there was no punk giving me a hard time, and nobody got dead. It was just an age-old love story. So what gives with all the buzz about this Shakespeare guy's tales when you can have the real thing?